Chosen:

Forever & A Day With My Brooklyn Bae

By: E. Shanie

D1566225

Kalen

My little cousin SJ was turning eighteen, and the fam went all out for this shit. I had no plans on showing up because all these people were going to be younger than I was. However, SJ hit me up asking if I could show up because his little shorty's moms weren't going to let her come alone. I didn't get why she couldn't come to a party, but he told me that she didn't tell her mother that the party was at the club. Anyway, he told me ole girl sister was some uptight chick, and he needed me to entertain her.

Me out of all people to entertain some damn nerd was going to be interesting. I didn't tell Kalyla about it because I didn't want anyone to know about it. Also, Kalyla had been on some other shit, so I didn't have time for all that. I sat in my little section with my feet kicked up and a bottle of Henny taking in the view of all these kids doing these whack ass dances. SJ's little friend and her sister had thirty more minutes to arrive before I took my ass home.

As soon as the thought popped in my head, SJ was telling me to come down and meet them. I grabbed the bottle of Hennessy and made my way over to where my people were standing.

"Aye! So, this is my older cousin, Kalen. Kalen this is my girl Riah and her sister DiZarie!" SJ introduced as soon as I walked over.

"Your girl? You didn't tell me that. How you doing, beautiful?" I greeted.

The one he introduced as Riah smiled and shyly waved back to me. Shorty was a pretty dark skin girl, but her sister, I damn sure wasn't expecting shorty to look like this. I thought shorty was going to come with her hair undone and some big clothes on by the way that SJ described her. Shorty right here was something completely different though. She had on a pair of tight black jeans and a white fitted belly shirt. Around her shapely hips, she had those beads I saw Kalyla wear before. I couldn't tell if she had a weave in her head, but it was long as shit. She had a pretty face too. This was going in a completely different direction.

"Hey, DiZaire. I'm glad you're not ugly since this nigga has me on babysitting duty," I joked with my hand out.

"Please don't get her started on looks. I am not in the mood to hear her rant right now. Sissy, please enjoy your time, and we won't even stay the whole night," her sister pleaded.

"I'm not a kid, so I don't need babysitting. You can have fun, but never again. I didn't know it was a party filled with little kids," DiZarie complained.

"You are only two years older, so please stop. Hang out with his cousin, and when you're ready to leave, we can," her sister said before SJ pulled her away from us.

"Aye, follow me this way," I instructed.

DiZarie looked back in the direction that her sister went in before self-consciously pulling at her shirt and following behind me. I took her back to the corner I was ducked off in and now that we were alone shit, got awkward.

"So, what's up with you, DiZarie? Why you look so uptight?"

"I am not uptight. I am just uncomfortable. I normally don't dress like this, and I'm trying to be nice for my sister. Also, my mother told me I had to. I just want to put my hair up in a ponytail and just chill," she groaned slouching in the seat, crossing one leg over the other.

"You look good. I have a rubber band so that you can put your hair up," I offered.

She snatched up the rubber band so fast and swooped all her hair up into a ponytail. I guess my questions about if her hair was real or not was answered. As soon as her hair went up, she completely relaxed. Damn, she was definitely a beautiful girl.

"Why are you staring at me?" she questioned, rolling her eyes.

"Man, go on with all that shit. I am not staring at you. You're just not what I expected that's all."

"What the hell did they tell you about me? Everyone loves to over exaggerate. I just love to be looked at for my mind, but not my body," she said, folding her arms over her exposed stomach.

"Well, being weird and acting like an ummm…"

"Nigga, I know you weren't about to call me a bitch!" She snapped, turning her head in my direction.

"Yo, you wilding. I wouldn't call a female a bitch. My mother and my Annie would fuck me up." I laughed.

"Who's Annie? That's your girlfriend? You're dating a white girl?" She questioned with her face frowned up.

"My Annie. The fuck you mean my girlfriend. If you want to know if I'm single that's all you have to do is ask, no need to assume."

"You keep talking about my Annie. What is an Annie, and why is she yours?"

"Everybody has one. I don't get why you're confused right now?" I let out.

"I mean everyone doesn't have one because I don't. Do you like find an Annie out on the street or what? How do I go about getting me my own personal Annie?" She asked sarcastically.

"Man, take yo ass on somewhere. Does your mother or father have a sister? That's your Annie," I explained.

"Nigga, you're talking about auntie, YOUR AUNTIE! Where the hell did you get Annie from?" She laughed.

Her smile was contagious. Her dimples and pretty white teeth had a nigga smiling and shit.

"That's what I've always called her," I explained.

"You are a little bit too old to still be calling her that. I'll let it go though because it's none of my business," she said, letting out a little laugh.

"Don't try to play me. You want a drink?" I questioned, holding up the bottle of Hennessey.

"Sure. We took an Uber here," she said, reaching out to take the cup.

This night definitely wasn't going to go that bad.

****

"Shorty, you shouldn't have drunk that much if you can't hold your liquor," I said laughing walking with DiZarie and her sister to the door.

"First off I am not drunk. I just feel nice. Like if you say Zarie do a cartwheel, I am ninety-five percent sure that I can do one. Besides, I can't leave without my sister," Zaire pointed out.

"Shorty, she's right beside you." I laughed.

"Zarie, I see you enjoyed yourself with Mr. Kalen." Her sister laughed doing some dance.

"Stop being embarrassing, Riah. Let's go," Zarie said, not trying to make eye contact with me.

"Man, wait right here. I was going to have my grandfather's driver take me home. They can take the two of you home."

"Ohhh Riah, his grandfather has a driver," she said in some funny accent.

"Man, bring your ass on Zarie. Where do y'all live, Riah?" I questioned, helping them into the car.

She called out her address, and I got into the back seat with them after giving Mel the address.

"I swear I cannot wait until I get out of these clothes. I'm going to have to talk to De because I can't do this again." Zarie complained, pulling at her pants and shirt.

"Who the hell is De?" I questioned.

"My daddy. Who else would that be, Kalen?" She questioned, rolling her eyes.

"Zarie, I'm telling daddy you called him De," Riah joked.

"You are always snitching Riah, always snitching. Momma is going to be mad because I am washing my hair when I get home. Momma spent four, almost five hours straightening my hair. She might be upset for a little while, but she will get over it, right?" Zarie asked, talking her hair out of the ponytail.

"Is this your hair or is this a weave?" I asked, reaching out to touch her hair.

"Ew, didn't your Annie teach you not to put your hands in a woman's hair? This is not a weave. You need to chill out," Zarie called out, slapping my hand away from her hand.

"Aye, where are you from?" I asked, laughing.

"North Carolina," she sang with her eyes closed.

She was gone right now. Those drinks definitely loosed her ass up because she wasn't acting like this when I first met her ass. When we pulled up in front of their crib, I was surprised. Maybe our lives weren't so different because their house damn sure showed they had money. Maybe they weren't in the same business, but whatever their parents were doing made them some money.

"Thank you so much for helping us get home," Riah said, climbing out and helping her sister out the car.

"Damn Riah, I do know how to walk. Kalen, I guess it was nice to meet you," Zarie said as she pulled at her jeans.

I couldn't help but look at her ass jiggle in her pants. Damn, and to think she said she doesn't dress like this all the time. At least I got to see that ass once. Zarie threw two fingers up and made her way towards the front door.

"It doesn't matter what the situation is she will find a way to embarrass me. At least she looks fine as fuck while doing it," Riah said, shaking her head as she gathered their things.

"Let her live. At least she loosened up some." I laughed.

"Yeah, I guess so. Thank you so much for the ride, Kalen. It was nice to meet you," she said, smiling.

"No problem. Aye, give me your sister's number," I called out, pulling out my phone.

She stared at me for a second before taking my phone and putting in Zarie's number.

"Don't try to play my sister, because if you do, you will have to see me. My family is my heart, and I don't play about them," Riah threatened.

"I'm not trying to do no bullshit. I really want to get to know shorty. From the talks we had tonight, she seems cool as fuck," I replied.

"Yeah okay. Thanks again, Kalen," Riah let out before running towards the front door that Zarie left wide open.

I stood out front waiting for Riah to get into the house and close the door before getting in the car so that I could head over to Kalyla's apartment. I haven't seen or spoken to her annoying ass since earlier, so I had to drop in on her. While I sat in the back seat, Zarie was on my mind. I decided to shoot her a text and see if she would respond to a nigga in the morning.

Me: *Not on no creep shit, but I want you to know that you were fine as fuck today. It was nice to meet you, and I learned a lot about you tonight— one being that you can't handle your liquor.*

Me: *By the way, this is Kalen. Your sister gave me your number.*

The whole night I spent talking to DiZarie, I became more interested in knowing who she was. She didn't forget to remind me that she was more than just her body, and if she weren't drinking, she would tell me why the way I looked at her as wrong on so many levels. That alone had me wondering about her. She kind of reminded me of Kalyla by the way she acted. I already sent her a text, so the ball was definitely going to be in her court.

Kalyla

Y ou would think that Kalen and I having two different apartments would give him the hint of us not having to be around each other all the time, but no. I couldn't even sleep in today because of his damn phone. Kalen slept peacefully next to me with his hand in his basketball shorts while I sat up with an attitude. I reached over on his side of the bed to grab his phone. I unlocked his phone and went through his notifications.

I rolled my eyes as I scrolled through all the normal bitches that blow Kalen up on the regular, but there was someone new here. Who the fuck was *DiZarie?* I clicked on the message, and I saw what he texted her. I sucked my teeth and looked down at a sleeping Kalen trying to refrain from slapping him. Who the fuck was this new girl?

DiZarie: *Umm, funny how you tried not to be a creep, but dead came off as a creep. I hope you know complimenting my looks does nothing for me. I am more than my appearance.*

DiZarie: *Oh, by the way, this is Zarie. The real Zarie Lol* *Photo added*

I clicked on the picture to make it bigger, and I was confused. Who the hell was this girl and why was she sending pictures of herself to Kalen. I wasn't a hater, so I couldn't even call ole girl ugly. The picture she sent you could tell she didn't have on any makeup. Her hair was all over the place in kinky natural curls. She was a pretty girl with skin that resembled cinnamon. She smiled in the picture sticking up her middle finger.

I don't know why but this whole interaction bothered the fuck out of me. I decided to check through his phone to see what else was new. Kalen was supposed to be my best friend, and he didn't tell me about some DiZarie chick. Where the hell did he meet her? Something told me to go to his pictures, and when I did, I was confused as fuck. Kalen went to SJ's party last night and got with one of his little friends. Damn, that was a new low for Kalen.

"Did you find whatever you were looking for?" Kalen asked, laughing.

I jumped to the sound of his voice and threw his phone at him.

"Don't do that! I was just checking who the fuck was blowing you up. I couldn't even get any good sleep because of your phone going off nonstop," I complained.

"My bad, man. Who was it?" he asked, placing his phone on the nightstand next to the bed.

"A bunch of your usual, but I saw someone new in there. Who's DiZarie? You fuckin' with little girls now, Kalen?" I sassed.

"Oh shit, Zarie hit me back?" He asked hype as hell.

"Oh, you have a nickname for her and everything. Damn, when you meet shorty?"

"I met her last night at SJ's party. She's SJ girlfriend's older sister. She seemed cool as fuck, and the fact that she's bad as fuck added to it," he said as he went through his messages.

"Damn! She looks good even without the straight hair and makeup. She looks good as fuck." Kalen amped.

"Aight nigga, calm down. I know you've seen pretty girls before," I said, rolling my eyes.

"You jealous? What the fuck is going on with you, Lyla?" Kalen asked, getting up from my bed and going into the bathroom.

"Ain't nobody jealous. I just never saw you this hype about a girl! Shit, I didn't even meet her, and you trying to run to the altar," I let out.

"Man, go on with that shit. At the end of the day, I'm a nigga and shorty bad as fuck. Lyla, you didn't see what I saw last night. Thick hips, ass, a pretty face, nice teeth, and real hair. Then to top it off shorty is not a bum bitch either. If I decide to fuck with her on that level, I don't have to hear my mother and everyone talk about her using me for money and shit. I'm pretty sure you would like her too, so that's a good thing too," he called out from the bathroom.

"I doubt it," I said lowly to myself.

"Aye, what do you have planned today?" Kalen asked as he walked back into my room.

"Nigga, did you wash your hands?" I questioned, cutting my eyes at him.

"Yeah, man! Now what are your plans?" he asked, walking out of my room altogether.

I scrambled to my feet and followed behind him to see his greedy ass wasn't doing shit but going through my kitchen trying to eat up my shit.

"We have that family meeting in like two hours at P. Storm's house. After that, I'm not doing anything. Why?"

"Oh shit! I forgot about that damn meeting. Let me go get dressed. Aye, I'll be back, and then we can leave!" he called out before walking out the door of my apartment.

I rolled my eyes and went back into my room so that I could get dressed. I looked at the other side of my room and saw Kalen's shit all on my floor. He would just leave his shit on my floor like he had a damn maid over here.

****

"I tell you all a time to be here, and I expect everyone to show up on time. What time were you all supposed to be here?" P. Storm barked.

I sat there with my eyes wide and looked around the table at everyone else whose facial expressions matched mine. He never went off on us. It was mostly towards the adults, but right now, he looked pissed.

"Daddy, I have a whole house of kids to deal with. We are here now, so what's up?" Auntie Ny said.

The way P. Storm gaze cut in her direction, I knew she chose the wrong time to get smart.

"Well, you and your whole damn house were supposed to be here Nyrae, so I don't want to hear the shit. I give out orders for a reason. When I tell y'all to do something, I expect you all to fuckin' follow the orders!" he barked.

"ShaKeem, get to the point. They were late. We can't change it now. Go on with this damn meeting, Keem." Grandma Rayven cut in.

"Don't tell me how to speak to my kids and grandkids. One day y'all are going to regret not listening to me. I'm not going to be around forever," he lectured.

"What's going on here? Is something wrong with you?" Kalen cut in.

"No, but with the business that I run, anything can happen to me at any given moment, and I see that no one in my family is ready or capable to take over for me," P. Storm let out.

"Whoa, why didn't you come to me for that?" Auntie Ny cut in.

"You left this shit alone," Uncle Symeer cut in.

"I'm the next best option. I know he's not looking for one of these young ones to take over. That wouldn't make sense at all. They haven't even gone into training," Auntie Ny argued.

"Nyrae and Lou, we will have a separate talk. You all are here because it's time for my grandkids to go into training. You all may not want to go into the business, but you have to go into training."

"My kids are good. They can go through your training, but mine are good to go. With Symeer still out there and my past, I have been training my girls and SJ," Auntie Ny announced.

I know she took Kalen and me to the gun range a few times, but we never had an official training. Besides, I didn't plan on doing what they did for a living.

"What is this training for?" Ja'Nyla asked.

I swear her attitude and the way she looked was a fuckin' mirror image of Auntie Ny. She hated when anyone compared her to her mother, but they act just alike.

"Training for the family business. Y'all are a little too young for assignments, but you need to be prepared." P. Storm informed.

"We are eighteen. What age can we start? If y'all let SJ do it, y'all have to let us do it. He's the youngest out of the three of us. We might be hood triplets, but we're older," Ja announced.

"Your mother didn't tell me if y'all planned on going to school or what," P. Storm let out.

"I plan on making money. If I gotta drop bodies to do it, I'm with it. There's money to be made, so I don't have time to sit in someone's classroom," Ja said, smiling.

"Oh and I speak for my other halves as well," She called out pointing at Syn and SJ.

"Wrong! They all will be doing online classes since they don't want to be on campus. They aren't doing assignments until I say so," Auntie cut in.

"Nah ma, I'm grown now. I should be able to make my own decisions," Ja replied.

"You're not ready for all of that," Auntie said, shutting her down.

"I am the spawn of Nyrae and Symeer, so I should be good," Ja said, laughing.

"I told you to stop saying that shit. You make us sound like the devils or some shit talking about spawn, but shit, that don't mean nothing. Bullets don't give a fuck who your parents are. Y'all aren't doing assignments until I say so," Auntie dismissed.

"Aight, so look. I'm giving y'all options now. I'm getting older and shit ain't the same. I use to have the top hitters in the game. After Nyrae and Lou decided to walk away, I had a little good team, but nobody compared to them two. So right now, I've been considering shutting my shit down and just have y'all still train because of course being the offspring of Storm, you will always be a target. Then I will just help y'all build business. We have to keep money flowing in the family. Or the young ones are going to take this shit serious and put the fam back on top and be the best hitters out here," P. Storm announced.

I was down for opening a business. I don't think I can go around killing people. Shit, I love my fam, but I'm not about that life. We can do training for protection, but I planned on opening up a business, and I hope Kalen was on the same page.

"I'm ready to be the best. When does training start?" Kalen as hype as fuck.

"Whoa, we didn't even talk about it," I called out finally speaking up.

"What is there to talk about? My whole family has done it. I'm only following in the footsteps of the fam," Kalen said, looking at me.

"Training starts next week, and that's for everyone. I need your decisions once y'all have successfully completed training. You all can leave," P. Storm said before getting up from the table to leave.

"What kind of shit is daddy on? He's walking around like he some kind of Don or some shit? He knows I hate being dismissed,"

Auntie Ny said, cutting her eyes at the door that P. Storm just walked out of.

Oh, this was a little too much. Kalen and I definitely had some talking to do. There was no way in hell he really thought us doing hits for a living was the way to go.

DiZarie

I finally agreed to meet up with Kalen again. It was cool texting him and talking to him on the phone because he could make me laugh, but for some reason, I didn't want to meet up with him again. He saw the Zarie that was forced out of her comfort zone. What if he didn't like the Zarie that hated getting her hair done and getting dressed?

"Just let me fix your hair," my mother voiced bringing me out of my thoughts.

I was in my room sitting on the floor with my hair all over my head trying to figure out a lie to tell him so that I can cancel this meetup.

"No! This will be yet another time he sees me, and I'm not comfortable. I should just save us both the trouble and tell him that I'm not going," I called out as I started to text Kalen.

Just when the thought of canceling on him yet again popped in my head, he was FaceTiming me. I answered the FaceTime and waited for his face to appear on the screen.

"Aye, hold up. I told you I was going to go meet up with my girl," he told someone in the back.

"I'm not your girl, Kalen," I cut in laughing.

"Aye don't say that shit while I'm around my people. They're going to think I'm delusional," he joked.

"Because you are. Where are you?" I asked as a girl popped up on my screen with her face all frowned up.

"Man, move Lyla. The fuck you doing? Aye, I'm about to leave my Annie house. Are you ready or you're going to come up with another excuse?" he asked, staring me down.

"Stop trying to act like you know me." I laughed, rolling my eyes.

"I know that I've been trying to chill with you and you have a million and one excuses on why you can't. I've been going to training, and I still make time to talk to yo nappy head ass. The least you can do is entertain a nigga for a little, even if you want to be just friends."

"Ohh, I like him. Don't cancel your date, DiZarie," my mother cooed in the background.

"Who was that?" Kalen questioned.

"My mother," I groaned, turning the phone in her direction.

"How are you? My name is Kalen," Kalen greeted.

"Ew, what are you doing? I did not tell you to introduce yourself to my mother." I laughed.

"You dead wanted me to meet your moms. Now come on. I can come get you, or I can meet you there. A nigga about to go to the zoo for you so you better not stand me up," he pressed.

"And are you coming by yourself or are you trying to get me to meet that girl?" I questioned.

"I wasn't going to bring that up. But yeah, she's coming, and I'm bringing Zobie so that you won't feel awkward."

"Kalen, I don't think it's a good idea," I let out.

"Come on, man. You want me to pick you up?" he inquired.

"I'll meet you there," I replied before disconnecting the call.

"Let me do your hair!" my mother pleaded.

"Nope, I'll comb it, but I'm not straightening my hair again," I declined.

"Yes, you are! You can dress however you want, but you won't show up with your hair like this. You need to get used to getting your hair done again. Your daddy let you get away with this shit for a long time, but you are twenty years old Zarie. It's time to act like a big girl," my mother scolded as she walked out of my room.

"Ma, I don't have all day for you to do my hair. He's already leaving to go there," I complained.

"Who's already leaving?" my daddy asked, walking out of their bedroom.

"I have a somewhat date to go to, and your wife keeps trying to do my hair."

"Wait, I'm still confused on the whole date thing. When did you start dating, Zarie? I just started allowing your sister to date!" my daddy stressed.

"Daddy, I am twenty years old. I think it's okay for me to date now. Besides, I don't even think it will go anywhere anyway," I admitted.

"Wait why? That nigga cheating already? Don't have me fuck that nigga up, Zarie," my father said with his face scrunched up.

"No, I just don't think he would like the real Zarie. He acts like he's into what I have to say and doing dorky stuff I like to do, but even y'all say that I'm annoying. He's not going to want to put up with me for long."

"First off, if he doesn't like the real you, then he's a nigga that doesn't deserve your time. You may be a little annoying, but you are amazing, and if that little nigga can't see that, then he doesn't need to be around you," he said, pulling me into a hug.

"Thanks, daddy. Can you tell your wife to stay away from my hair?" I whined.

"Man, Ra let her live her life. You need to be worried about your husband and not her hair," my daddy scolded.

I took that as m cue to go on back to my room and get ready. I was about to see Kalen again. I had to look decent at least.

****

You know when I hyped myself up earlier, I did not expect for me to get scared once I pulled up to the Bronx Zoo. I didn't think I looked too bad right now. My mother straightened my hair again only because I didn't feel like arguing with her ass about my hair anymore.

I decided to put on a pair on black skinny jeans that had rips in them. On my feet, I had on the Retro Jordan ones that were half red and black and half red and white. I couldn't decide on a shirt, so I chose to wear an old school Chicago Bulls jersey. My mother wanted me to change so badly, but I thought I looked good.

"Aye, over here!" I heard Kalen call out.

I turned in the direction of his voice, and I started laughing. I swear this boy want to be like me so bad.

"What do you have on?" I questioned, laughing.

"Mann, this shit is crazy." He laughed

"Kalen, you didn't have this on when I spoke to you earlier. Why did you change your clothes?" I questioned.

"Well because…"

"Kalen, you couldn't wait until we got out the car too, damn!" a girl snapped behind him.

My whole demeanor changed when I saw that me and ole girl had the exact same outfit on. Kalen jersey and shoe color were different, but me and ole girl had the same outfit on. I was over this whole thing right now. I was ready to go home right now. The way shorty looked at me and the fact that Kalen thought this shit was funny had me pissed.

"I'm about to go," I gritted, pulling at my jersey.

"We can change jerseys if you would like," he offered.

"Why, so you and your girlfriend can be twins? I don't know what kind of shit y'all on, but I'm not the one. Shorty gives me a bad vibe, and I'm not with it," I informed him.

"Man, please don't be one of them girls," he groaned.

"One of what girls? A girl that tells you how it is? I don't have time for the bullshit. You cool people in all, but I'm not about to chill with shorty like we cool."

"It can't be the truth if you didn't even try to get to know her. Come on. I think you're cool as fuck too, but shit is not going to work if you can't accept Kalyla," he stated.

"Nigga, if I can't be friends with you because of shorty, then you need to think again. It's more than just a friendship between the two of you."

"Man, don't do that Kalyla," he cut in.

I had a meme moment. The meme where the white guy had to blink and cock his head back because he couldn't believe what was being said. That was literally me right now. This nigga really just called me Kalyla. I know damn well I don't look like that damn girl. I've been wanting to go to the zoo, so my ass wasn't leave, but I know for sure I wasn't about to chill with that nigga. I didn't even say anything else to him. I just walked off. I paid my way into the zoo, and I went to explore. Whatever was supposed to happen between Kalen and me vanished in the parking lot.

I cannot believe I even showed up to this bullshit ass date or whatever the fuck this is supposed to be.

"Aye, DiZarie, hold up shorty." I heard behind me.

I glanced over my shoulder and saw it was his friend running in my direction. I didn't have a problem with him, so I stopped and allowed him to catch up with me.

"So, I didn't get a chance to officially meet you. I'm Zobie," he greeted, sticking his hand out.

"I'm, DiZarie. I mean you know that already. Nice to meet you." I laughed and shook his hand.

"So, are you going to chill with us, or are you going to enjoy all of this by yourself?" He asked as we walked side by side.

I took the time to take him in. Zobie's look definitely didn't match his name. I don't even know what kind of nigga should have the name Zobie, but the one that walked next to me was definitely good looking, well in my opinion. Zobie stood at a height of six feet even or six one at the most. Nice smooth cocoa colored skin that had a nice gleam to it out in the sun. He had a nice little mustache and then a little patch of chin hair. His hair was cut in a low cut, and he had the little kinky curls going on. When he smiled, I was able to see his pretty teeth. Maybe Kalen wasn't the one I should be checking for.

"Hello, you good?" He asked, bringing me back to the conversation.

"I'm not with all that or whatever the hell they have going on. Kalen seems cool but ole girl, I'm not with."

"The two of them have known each other for a long time. The both of them are very overprotective of each other," Zobie tried to explain.

I cut my eyes at him and gave him a simple eye roll. I kept strolling through because I had one section on my mind. I wanted to see the aquatic birds!

"You not going to wait for them?" Zobie asked, laughing.

"No, I didn't plan on waiting doing anything with y'all. I was just going to enjoy this by myself," I admitted.

"You're stubborn, shorty. You really have to be around them just to see how they are around each other to completely understand." He tried to explain.

"Why do I have to understand their situation? I'm not even going to try to make y'all see it from my point of view. I'm about to enjoy this day by myself, and then I'm going on about my business. I'm good on him and his best friend," I announced.

"Damn, so that's it?" Zobie inquired.

"Yeah! It was nice meeting you, Zobie," I said nicely before walking away from him.

This was a dub, but I got to go to the zoo.

Kalen

How in the fuck did all of this go wrong? The whole dressing alike was not planned, and it does nothing but prove my point of her and Kalyla being alike more than either one would like to admit. It's been about two weeks since SJ party, and since then, I've been keeping in touch with Zarie. If it wasn't texting, then we were on FaceTime or on the phone. Today was supposed to be the day where Kalyla met her and hopefully, liked her.

That didn't turn out like that at all. All it took was for Zarie to see Kalyla clothes for everything to go south. I like Zarie, but I wasn't about to be with no female that couldn't accept everyone in my life. These girls might not like Kalyla, but she isn't going anywhere.

"Aye, what did she say?" I asked Zobie as he walked back over to us.

"Why does it matter what she said? I don't like her attitude. You can definitely do better, and shit, I've seen you with better." Kalyla stayed with her face frowned up.

"But I like her. Man, y'all bugged the fuck out," I said, shaking my head.

"Well, shorty is not feeling it. She doesn't fuck with Kalyla, and she doesn't care what kind of friendship y'all have. I tried to explain. If you like her saying that you have to accept Kalyla or you're walking away is not going to work. She's going to throw the deuces up let you walk away," Zobie informed, laughing.

"Yo, she dead ass said that shit?"

I mean I had to know that she was the type of female. Shorty love giving me a hard time.

"Yeah man. Shorty is not fuckin' with it. I'm not going to tell you I told you so, but nigga you will learn." Zobie stayed.

"Wait what the fuck is that supposed to mean, Zobie?" Kalyla asked with an attitude.

"This nigga likes ole girl, and he bought you out of all people along with him today. Nigga, you should have gotten to know shorty more before trying to connect both worlds, especially around her," Zobie let out.

"I'm not the one that's the problem," Kalyla disputed.

"You will never like a girl he goes out with, and that's probably because you want that spot. I know the both of you will say no, but one of you is lying about it. You missed out on some real shit. Ole girl seems cool as fuck just from the little conversation that we had. You have to come correct with that one," Zobie schooled.

I was stuck right now. I don't know if I should stay here with Kalyla because at the end of the day she's my best friend. Then you have Zarie who I'm definitely interested in, and she doesn't even want to try to get to know Kalyla. I couldn't let her walk around the damn zoo by herself.

"Aye, I'm going to chill with her for a bit," I announced.

"Are you serious right now?" Kalyla asked with her mouth hung open.

"Yeah, man. This was supposed to be us hanging out together, and this definitely didn't go as planned. I'm not about to let her walk around here by herself," I replied.

"Wow, Kalen. You're really about to run behind that girl?" Kalyla said still not believing it.

"Man, bring ya crybaby ass on. Let that man live his life," Zobie said, grabbing her hand and walking in the opposite direction.

I walked over to the direction that I saw Zobie come from and pulled out my phone to call her. The phone rang for a little bit, and she sent a nigga to voicemail. She's really going to have me hem her ass up. A nigga is trying to do the right thing and chill with her ass. I shot a text to Zobie to see where the hell he last saw her ass, and he told me she went to see the aquatic birds section.

I went over to that section and walked through looking for her. Shorty was really sitting here enjoying this shit by herself. She was walking through with her phone out smiling ear from ear taking pictures of the animals and shit.

"You are a piece of work, Zarie," I said, walking up behind her.

She glanced over her shoulder but kept her attention on the penguins that were swimming in the water. She used her phone to zoom in to get a better look for her video.

"Are you really going to ignore me?" I questioned, moving closer to her.

"Can I get some room? I wanted to come here because I love animals. I don't like the whole idea of them being caged, but I love to look at all the beautiful animals. I don't have time to sit and argue with you about ya girl. That's one thing you will come to learn about Zarie. She will sit on her own self made throne. She doesn't argue or fight for a spot," she sassed still not even giving me her undivided attention.

"Why the fuck are you talking in third person?" I laughed.

"Whatever, Kalen. I want to enjoy my time today, so if you don't mind, excuse me," she said before walking off.

"Damn, this is supposed to be us spending time together and getting to know one another. Why you keep walking off."

"Listen your friend that came to talk to me knows how I feel about this. I'm good on it. What you and ole girl are trying to sell I'm not buying. The whole having to go through her, I'm not with. I would never come in between you and her because that's way before me. Personally, I just don't like the vibe that she gives off. I've heard the attitudes when we would talk on the phone, and you were around her. I saw the faces she would make when we were on FaceTime. Shorty doesn't know me, and she already has a preconceived notion about me. That's because she most likely feels like I'm stepping on her toes. Y'all got something going on?"

"What the fuck is with everyone saying that? I do not like her. We do not see each other in that light. I've known her since I was six. She's my best friend— well shit more like a sister that I never asked for." I admitted.

"Does she still feel the same way about you?" Zarie shot back.

Why the fuck has everyone been making that damn assumption? Kalyla and I have always been close! What the hell was changing now?

"Yes, she feels the same way," I argued.

"Okay. If we are going to be friends or if we are working on something here, she and I being around each other has to wait," she informed.

"Fine! We will ease that in."

I was definitely going to hear some shit from Kalyla after today. There was never a time where I went chasing behind a female. If they didn't fuck with Kalyla, I wasn't fuckin' with them, but here comes Zarie and shit is going in a different direction. This shit is going to be more stressful than I planned.

****

It's been a week since the zoo, and Kalyla was refusing to talk to me. I didn't see the problem, and she was making this into some bigger shit. We were now in training, and she decided to train with the twins and SJ instead of me. I don't see anything wrong with how I handled the situation. I told her I was feeling Zarie, and she wasn't even trying to go easy on it. Zobie tried to tell me that it was all my fault, but nah, I didn't see it the same way.

"Hey, why are you by yourself?" I heard from behind me.

I turned to see my mother and Annie walking in my direction loading up their guns.

"Kalyla's not fuckin' with me right now," I admitted as I shot at the target.

"Why?" My mother questioned as she began to set up her station.

"Put the gun down. I have to hear this," my Annie said hyped up.

I needed some advice, so I guess I can take a break. I placed my gun down and turned to face my moms and Annie. They both stood there looking like OGs with their arms folded waiting for me to talk.

"So, I met this girl," I started.

"Let me guess, you aren't going to fuck with her because Kalyla doesn't like her," my mother said, rolling her eyes.

Yeah, they were tired of this dance like a bunch of other people I'm sure.

"Nah, like a week ago I tried to get her and Kalyla in the same room and shit went wrong," I said, shaking my head.

"Where you meet this girl?" my Annie asked.

"She's SJ's girlfriend older sister." I smiled.

"Is she cute?" my mother asked.

I pulled out my phone and showed them the pictures that I secretly snapped of Zarie. Her thuggin' ass is always sticking her middle finger up in a picture, so I have to catch her ass off guard. They both stood close and flipped through the pictures with smiles on their face.

"Wait this is SJ girlfriend sister? They look nothing alike," my Annie pointed out.

"Anyway, that's Zarie. I don't know. It's something about her that keeps my attention. So last week I tried to get her to meet Kalyla. She had been told me that she didn't want to be around her. She claims she could tell that they weren't going to get along because of Kalyla acts when we are talking on the phone or when we FaceTime. I don't see a problem with it, but she's not having it. Anyway, back to last week. I finally got her ass to agree to meet up and chill with me again. She likes animals and shit like that, so she said she wanted to go to the zoo. Shit, she wanna go to the zoo, we going to the zoo. We get there, and we all dressed alike. I mean literally. Her and Kalyla had on the same outfit down to the shoes. None of this was planned, and I thought the shit was funny. Nah, she didn't think so! She was pissed off. We go back and forth because she's acting all confused on the reason why I decided to bring Kalyla along, and you know me. You have to accept Kylyla if you want something with me. I always get the girls with that.

They hear I'm not an option without her, and they straighten up for a while until I say fuck them. Shorty told me she was good on me and just walked away," I said to them and stopped talking so that they can tell me she was bugging.

"As she should. Continue," my Annie called out.

"Nah! She should have just tried to get to know her! But with her being stubborn, I ended having to choose. I decided to go after her instead of leaving the zoo with Kalyla. I don't know what it is about her, but she doesn't take my shit. Even after I went after her ass, she still tried to shut me down. Her ass going to tell me whatever Kalyla and I are trying to sell her she ain't buying. She's cool with trying to get to know me and be friends or see what's up with us, but she ain't about to go through Kalyla to do it. Zarie said she doesn't like Kalyla's vibe and she's not about to try and come between us because she understands that before her time. Anyway, she basically said that the way Kalyla acts has her feeling like maybe she's stepping on Kalyla's toes. She's not trying to take anyone else's spot. It had her asking if Kalyla and I had something going on. Anyway, of course, I denied it because I don't see Kalyla in that light, but she is my best friend. That right there will never change. Now I feel like I have to prove that shit to Zarie and get shit right with Kalyla," I expressed.

"Wait, I'm confused on what's Kalyla's problem?" my mother asked.

"She feels like I chose Zarie over her."

"Give her some space. She will get over it," my Annie concluded.

"Now so what's up with this girl? Are you trying to be serious with her? I want to meet her," my mother said, smiling.

"Let me FaceTime her so that y'all can hear how she acts. She's a geeky thug." I laughed deciding to FaceTime her.

The phone rang a couple of times before she finally answered.

"Riah, I'm going to punch you. Stop touching my shit. Hold on, Kalen. I swear you call at the wrong times."

"Ohh, Kalen. Are y'all kissing yet? Sissy, he is cute, and if you start being your weird, dorky self and run him off, I'm going to fight you. Loosen up some. Does he touch your butt?" Riah let out in the background.

"First off, if he doesn't like Zarie, and how she is normally? That nigga doesn't even deserve to look at my butt. Second, I don't have to show my ass to get some attention. Kalen's cool people but ummm he's occupied with his best friend," Zarie said, rolling her eyes.

"Don't do that," I cut in.

"Oh, he's on the phone for real. Um, don't mind what I said just now. Just remember what I said. You hurt my sister, and I hurt you," Riah said, giving me her little ass threat again.

"Um, he's just my friend. Get out of my room, Riah!" Zarie snapped.

"Oh, I'm just your friend now?" I asked once she finally gave me her attention.

"Yeah what else would you be Kalen? Also, why are you FaceTiming me now? I thought you were in training," she pointed out.

"I'm ya man, and we both know that. Now I am at training, but my moms and Annie want to see you."

"Ha funny. You are not my man, and you know that you already got a shorty. I don't fight over a nigga. Now, what did you tell them for them to want to see me? I know they don't want to meet your friends just because," she asked with a raised eyebrow.

"Man, we both know what's up, and you're just fronting because your sister might still be in the room. Now put a smile on that pretty face and say wassup to my moms and my Annie."

"YOUR AUNTIE!! Kalen, say it with me AUNTIE!" she corrected.

"Hell, nah I ain't saying that shit. It's Annie. The rest of the world is just taking forever to catch up." I laughed,

"A grown ass man and still refuse to say auntie correctly. Listen, I need to finish my homework because I have to get ready for tonight. Is there something you really needed?" she asked looking down and then back to the phone.

"Well, I said my moms and Annie wanted to see who you are, but that shit can wait. What are you getting ready for?"

My Annie and mother were trying to look all into the phone, and I was concerned more about what she had planned tonight and why she didn't tell me.

"I'm not getting ready right now. But if you must know, it's my birthday and going to a family dinner at Ruth Chris," she said, shaking her head.

"Damn, a nigga can't get an invite. Shit, why didn't I even know today was your birthday?" I inquired.

"Well because you are worried about the wrong things. Now, where are your moms and auntie? I have questions." She laughed.

"Nahhh, that can wait. You seriously never told me your birthday before," I pressed.

"I did, but obviously, you didn't pay attention to that conversation. I know your birthday," she replied.

"No, you don't," I argued.

"June twenty-fifth."

"Damn. You really told me that before? I don't remember that," I said aloud.

"Yeah because you were so busy pushing your friend down my throat. Now am I going to meet the fam or are we ending the conversation? Either way, I have homework to finish," she sassed rolling her eyes.

I was about to say something when my Annie snatch the phone from my hand. I didn't even bother to try and listen to what they were talking about because I honestly don't remember the conversation that we had where we even talked about birthdays. That is definitely something I should have remembered. That's probably why her ass was curving the fuck out of me.

"It was nice talking to you. Your such a beautiful soul. Happy Birthday, and I hope you enjoy your day," I heard before my phone was being shoved into my hands.

"Booooyy, I love Kalyla, but you fuckin' up with that one. If you plan on being with Kalyla, then leave that girl alone. If you want to take that girl seriously and want a relationship with her, it's time to make a line in the sand," my Annie schooled.

"Line in the sand?" I asked confusingly.

"Set boundaries with Kalyla. She is your best friend, not your lover. I hope you are making that clear to her because niggas love to lead a bitch on. Then she gets confused and bad things happen. Kalen, have a talk with Kalyla, a serious talk," my Annie warned.

I nodded my head because I heard her. I just don't think that Kalyla was going there with it. There were no romantic feelings between the two of us.

Kalyla

Normally when I have an attitude, Kalen would come and try to make it up to me. This nigga tried to come around me a couple of times, but he didn't want to admit that he was wrong for leaving me with Zobie and enjoying his time with that bitch. Never in our fifteen years of knowing each other has Kalen chosen another girl over me. What the hell is so special about this damn girl? Here comes this Zarie bitch and it's like I don't even matter. Now I'm forced to hang out with Zobie, or I'll chill with Laurel.

I try to stay away from her because I know what she wants and that's Kalen. I don't even know why her liking Kalen bothers me so much, but that shit annoys the fuck out of me. I can admit right now that shit was in a weird space for me. Like I've always been territorial over Kalen because I mean that's my best friend. That's also the nigga that didn't let shit happen that he wouldn't approve of. It's just that we are protective over each other. But lately, my shit 's been on a different level. I don't know what the fuck is going on with me.

"Aye are you done with your sets?" Kalen asked, rolling up behind me.

I rolled my eyes and continued to clean my gun as I took it apart to put it back in the case.

"What's wrong with you, Kalyla? You have to give in and talk to me soon," he said, taking a seat on the table next to where I was standing.

"Kalen I'm fine, and we have nothing to talk about," I cooed with my eye still fixed on the table.

"So why have you been ignoring me?"

"Because I don't feel like talking to you. You chose to run behind ole girl, and I'm choosing to chill out on you for a while," I informed him.

"Damn, I like shorty. That day was supposed to be me and her chilling, but I invited all of y'all. Then she already wasn't feeling you because of the shit you be doing when I talk to her, so I really should have waited it out for you two to meet."

"See and right there is where I have a problem. Since when was a bitch out there that would allow you to play me?" I spat and made sure he knew I was disgusted.

"I like her. She holds my attention, and I'm not going to push her to the side because she doesn't want to get to know you right now."

"That's what got the other bitches the walking slip. Here she comes, and now all bets are off, and it's fuck Kalyla. I never thought there would be a time where a bitch will have you shitting on me," I said, shaking my head.

I grabbed my case and took it to the lock in before grabbing my keys to leave. I cannot believe this nigga would say some shit like that. There was a time when that nigga would curve a female if I said I didn't like her damn shoes. Shit, let a bitch look at me wrong, and Kalen was doing damn juke moves to get out of their way because he wasn't fuckin' with them. Now, this damn Zarie girl says she doesn't want to be around me, and he's okay with it.

"Why the fuck does it bother you so much? Just like I want you to find a good nigga, I would hope you want the same for me!" Kalen called out, stopping me in my tracks.

"Yeah, but the difference is that I wouldn't let my nigga disrespect you or what we have," I argued.

"Lyla. Man, don't do that because you know I don't do that shit. I would never let the next person openly disrespect you. You have to admit you've been talking slick shit since you found out about shorty. Shit, you've come out the side of your neck more than once, and I never said anything. I'm also pretty sure that's why she doesn't want to be around your ass. If you were her, you would feel the same way," he argued.

I stood there with my arms folded across my chest with a full-blown attitude. Yeah, maybe his ass was right about that, but no bitch should ever come before me.

"Fine Kalen," I said, giving in.

"On some real shit, you already know what it is. You are my best friend. We in this shit fifteen years strong. She knows that, and she's fine with that. She's just not ready to try and go there with you, and I understand. You know you're hard to please," he said, smiling.

That stupid ass smile that always gets me. So, what if I'm hard to please.

"Kalen. Do whatever you're going to do with ole girl. I'm going to fall back," I said, smiling.

"Fall back means that we aren't going to be cool?" he asked.

"It just has to be different now. You're about to get a girlfriend, so I'm not really needed anymore," I let out.

I didn't believe shit. I was saying right now, but I was going to tell him that, so shit wouldn't be rocky between us. Yeah on the inside, I feel some type of way, but Kalen has been a part of my life, and I can't keep going on like this.

"Well, for me to make up to you, I want to take you out tonight. Just you, me, and Zobie go on out to Ruth Chris eat a nice steak and sit back so that we can talk and catch up," he proposed.

"Kalen, it's only been a week, but I will take free food," I said, smiling.

"Alright bet I'll knock on your door later so that we can go. I got some shit to do, and I'm going to take a nap," he informed me before pulling me into a hug.

I wrapped my arms around his waist and hugged him back. No matter how I felt about ole girl, I will always be there for Kalen. I don't know what was going on with my thinking towards Kalen, but it was nothing for me to get this shit right.

"I'll see you later, alright?" He questioned double checking with me.

"Yup we are on, and I'm ordering a big ass steak," I joked.

"Lyla, it's all on me." He laughed folding his arm out wide.

I just laughed and walked out of the warehouse. It was good to have Kalen hanging out with Zobie and me again. Well, it was mostly me who didn't want Kalen around, so now that I was going let that little fling with this DiZarie girl ride out.

****

Bestie Kalen: *In another hour, I'll be ready to head up out of there. So, if you're ready before then just come to my apartment, or I'll come get you so that we can leave.*

Me: *Well I'm finishing my hair, and I'll be ready to go. I'm going to kick back and watch some TV until it's time to go. You can just shoot me a text, and I'll meet you in the lobby.*

I finished up my hair and went into my living room with my feet kicked up so that I can wait until it was time to go. While I waited, I decided to text Zobie. The week I spent not talking to Kalen I bothered Zobie.

Me: *What's good, Zob?*

Zobbb: *Just getting off work. I almost had to lay my manager the fuck out. These niggas got me fucked up. I'll be in jail instead of making money.*

Me: *You and I both know you ain't about that life. Calm all that down before you be laid up in the hospital, and I have to put this training into use.*

Zobbb: *Shit, you can't buss a grape. What the hell you want brat?*

Me: *I just need someone to talk to until it's time for us to go to dinner.*

Zobbb: *I am not going.*

Me: *Yes, the hell you are. Kalen already said that you were coming. *tongue out emoji**

Zobbb: *Kalen ain't my daddy, nigga. Where the hell he plans on going?*

Me: *Ruth Chris. He out here trying to spend some money, and I'm going to let him LOL*

Zobbb: *I honestly think you owe dinner, but I'll settle for that nigga buying. Why didn't he tell me?*

Me: *I don't know he probably did, but I know you are famous for not checking your phone.*

Zobbb: *Oh, never mind. He actually did text me.*

Me: *As always, you never check your messages.*

Kalen: *I'm ready. Meet me down in the lobby.*

I didn't even check to see if Zobie texted me back I just slipped my phone into my bag, and I was ready to go. I locked up my place and got on the elevator to meet Kalen in the lobby.

****

We were now seated, and I wanted to leave. Kalen claims he didn't know that his new little girlfriend was going to be at the same restaurant, but hell nah, this isn't a coincidence. I definitely don't believe that shit. Since he spotted her in this damn restaurant with her people, his eyes have been fixated on the table.

"Did you seriously bring me here so that you can see that bitch? Kalen, I thought you were taking me out to say sorry," I complained.

"Aye, watch ya mouth. What did I tell you about him and that girl?" Zobie chastised, cutting in.

"Zobie, he could have left me out of it. I said I wasn't going to be in the way, but to show up with me knowing she was going to be here is fucked up," I groaned.

"Nah! That wasn't my intentions," Kalen lied.

"Well, no matter how he meant it, push that girl out of your head because she's clearly not worried about neither one of y'all," Zobie said, pointing in the direction of the table.

I swear I wanted to laugh. Here this nigga is taking her side over me and shorty has a whole other nigga. The way she got excited when that nigga walked over to the table made me smile. Kalen was getting what he deserved. He chooses that bitch over me, and now she's smiling in another nigga's face.

"Who the fuck is that?" Kalen snapped, standing up from the table.

"Shit, it's obviously her nigga. Look at how they are hugged up," I egged on.

"She definitely has me fucked up!" He snapped, storming off to the table.

"What the fuck was that?" Zobie asked pointing in the direction that Kalen walked off in.

"What did you want me to do? This was bound to happen since he thought it was a good idea to show up to the same place his bitch was having dinner. It's a good thing he saw it for himself."

"All this shit is about to go wrong, and that's because you egged that shit on. That man can be a family member, and you don't even care because you're so worried about having Kalen to yourself. Are you in love with him?" Zobie asked.

"Whaaat? No, why would you ask me something like that?" I scoffed.

Zobie cut his eyes at me and just shook his head. What the hell was he talking about?

DiZarie

So today I turned twenty-one, and I was out with the fam celebrating the greatness that is Zarie. In the back of my head, I felt some kind of way because Kalen admitted to not remembering my birthday. Yeah, we talked about it once, but shit, I remembered his, so why didn't he remember mine?

"So about this boyfriend I heard you had," my daddy announced as we all sat at the table.

Everyone at the table eyes fell on me as my mouth dropped open.

"Wait, you have a boyfriend? When did this happen? Is that why you're dressing differently?" My little brother Dyaire pressed.

At thirteen years old he thought he was older than me and could tell me what to do. He was sadly mistaken though.

"Daddy, why are you telling my business, and he's not my boyfriend," I groaned, covering my face.

"That's not what ya momma and Riah told me. I want to meet this boy too. I don't need you out here fuckin' and falling in love," my daddy called out.

"Oh hell nah! Who said you could fall in love. I thought I was your favorite uncle. How could I not know you found a nigga?" Uncle Juju cut in.

"Uncle Juju, please don't listen to them. I've been talking to a guy, but I mean it's nothing serious. I'm free to do as I please," I replied.

"Just to let that nigga know he gotta see me before he gets anything poppin' with you," Uncle Juju said with his face all frowned up.

"Like Zarie having a boyfriend is so unbelievable. I am so happy that you met this guy because now she doesn't complain when I ask to do her hair. She's showing off that figure for the world to see!" My mother let out excitedly as her, my sister and Auntie Saderia squealed in excitement.

"Listen, I really feel like y'all are over exaggerating right now. Kalen is fun to talk to, and I don't know. Shoot, I really don't know.

I'm just living my life. I am not claiming anyone, and no one is claiming me," I informed them.

"Aye, what's good family? Sorry, I'm late," my little cousin Jashuan said, walking into the restaurant.

I jumped out of my seat to embrace my favorite and only little cousin.

"Why are you late?" I quizzed.

"Basketball practice. I'm here though, and we about to turn up. You're twenty-one, so we about to get lit!" Shaun amped.

"Jashuan, don't have me beat your ass," Auntie Saderia cut in.

He laughed and took a seat next to me. The waiter came and placed our drinks in front of everyone and then took Jashuan's drink order before leaving again.

"Damn, I know I forgot what today is, but shit, you only told me once. How you got another nigga going out to family dinners and shit. Was this nigga ya boyfriend this whole time? You got a nigga out here telling my Annie I got a girl and shit. She's a little dorky, but she got a hint of thug life to her and shit, but the whole time shorty already got a nigga!" Kalen snapped, walking over to my table.

I didn't even know what to say, so I sat there shocked with my mouth just hung open.

"Who the fuck is this nigga?" My daddy snapped as all the men at the table stood up in defense.

"Okayyy, so this is so awkward right now!" I squealed as I jumped up from my seat to stand in front of Kalen.

"Zarie, you got some damn nerve to talk about this is awkward!" Kalen snapped from behind me.

"Nigga, the nerve of you!" I snapped, turning around.

He stood there with his handsome face all scrunched up and a clear attitude like I was in the wrong. I rolled my eyes and mushed him as hard as I could.

"Nigga, how did you know I would be at this one?" I questioned.

He looked around me, and I knew it was nobody but Riah.

"Riah, stop telling my business! He didn't know where for a reason. Now back to you. How dare you come to a family get together with a fuckin' attitude. You are not my nigga. I don't care what you told your AUNTIE or ya moms nigga. If you can't remember a conversation pertaining to our birthdays, it says a lot!" I snapped.

"Hell nah! You told me once, and it was like two days after we met! REMEMBER YOU ONLY TOLD ME ONCE. Why can't you be like a normal female and drop hints that ya birthday is coming up," he complained.

"I remembered yours! But you know what Kalen, trying to check me isn't the right move. You need to take a hint," I sassed.

I don't even know where I was going with my rant right now.

"Oh, what's the hint?" He asked.

He stood in a defensive stance getting closer into my personal space.

"Kalen I'm not playing with you!" I warned.

"Hell nah. I ain't playing with you either. Who is that nigga? You like them young like that? The nigga looks like he's no more than seven. What kind of shit you on?" he questioned, pointing towards Jashuan.

"Do you know who he is? Assuming really makes you look like an ass, Kalen. You ruined my birthday dinner because you're jealous and let me add jealous for no reason. We are not together, so you shouldn't be worried about my other niggas."

"Man, why are you making this shit harder than it has to be. We both know you're feeling me, and we already know how I feel about you. I'm tired of playing with you Zarie, and honestly, I feel disrespected right now. Instead of you tell ole boy to leave and letting me have a seat at the table, you want to argue."

"Kalen, leave!" I stressed.

"Nah."

"So, this is the nigga that has you switching up?" My daddy asked, walking over to us.

"I am not switching up. But since he wants to make a big scene and ruin my birthday dinner, AND NOT SHOW UP WITH A GIFT, I'll introduce him to everyone. Kalen, this is my mother Raniya, and you already know Riah. That's my little brother Dyaire, my Uncle

Juju, my AUNTIE Saderia, and my COUSIN Jashuan. Last but not least my daddy D'Eric. Everyone this is Kalen, I guess," I said, introducing everyone and rolling my eyes.

"Your cousin?" Kalen murmured.

"Yeah, my cousin. I don't know if I should be flatter that after almost a month of being friends you get this jealous or if I should be annoyed and block you," I gritted, squinting at him.

"Aye, little nigga, let me talk to you alone for a minute," my daddy demanded before walking to the exit with Uncle Juju getting out of his seat to follow them.

"Uncle Juju, please don't do this. Y'all nothing is going on with us. Besides I'm twenty-one." I argued, but they weren't trying to hear it.

"Maaaaa, please go get your husband," I groaned, sitting back in my seat.

"No, it was bound to happen. You like that boy, and they need to press him to make sure he ain't on no fuck shit. You don't want to end up pregnant while he still entertaining another female," my momma said, pointing to the table where Kalyla was giving me a death glare.

Why would he bring that bitch, and he knew I didn't fuck with her? To be petty, I waved over there, and Zobie gave me a head nod while mad ass Kalyla rolled her eyes. Kalen has another thing coming if he thinks I'm going to play these type of games with him. I am not the one or two! That nigga needs to go play somewhere else.

They left out of the restaurant to talk with Kalen, and the food came to the table. I wasn't even able to eat because I was so damn nervous right now. I don't know why Kalen couldn't just leave me alone. He's a distraction.

"Look like you weren't just staring at the door. Play with your food or something Zarie, damn!" My mother snapped from the end of the table.

"He's an alright guy, but I'm still not with it," my daddy stated before taking a seat.

"Wait. What?" I asked, standing up.

"Aye, young one, I told you. Stop playing games, DiZarie," my father scolded.

"What did you tell him? You know what I don't even care. Y'all ruined my birthday dinner, and for that, I'm over y'all. Kalen, you can leave," I said, shooing him off.

"Don't play with me. I'm going to make all this up to you. Get ready to cry, Zarie. You're about to fall for a nigga hard as fuck. GET READY!" Kalen called out loud as fuck backing away from the table.

"Kalen! I'm serious you better not. You need to stay away from me. The fact that you brought shorty with you to ruin my shit says a lot. You got her over there grilling my table and shit."

"Alright, I get that you're grown but watch ya mouth," my mother cut in.

"Ma! Now isn't the time!" I snapped.

"DiZarie!" She let out in a warning tone.

"Like I was saying, you can leave and leave me alone. Kalen, you just need to get a clue and don't ever contact me again."

"You dead ass right now? She isn't my girl, and her ass is not even in the running. Why Is every girl so damn concerned about her? It's us. I know it an awkward situation between the two of us, but I've known her since I was six. Since I was six and I've spent every day of my life with her ever since. Kalyla is my best friend, and that will never change. But, I do not have romantic feelings for her at all. I look at her as a sister nothing more," Kalen confessed.

"That's cool and all, but I'm still good on all of this. I don't have time for the confusing situation," I declined.

"You dead ass?" he questioned.

"Yup."

"Yeah okay. I'll see you around, DiZarie," he announced before walking off.

Everyone at the table looked at me in disbelief, but oh well. I am not the one to play these kinds of games with Kalen. He can tell me what he wants, but I know for sure that he planned on ruining my dinner, so why the fuck would he bring shorty knowing that I don't fuck with her. I don't care how close the two of them are. What matters when he's around me is that I don't rock with that girl. So, she should have never been with him. I needed a break from that nigga anyway.

Kalen

The nerve of Zarie to try and call it quits with a nigga. Since I popped up at that dinner, I haven't texted or called her. Her ass probably is chilling and living her life while I walked around pissed. I don't even know why I keep fuckin' up with her. Honestly, I should have just shown up with balloons and shit like I originally planned, but there was a part of me still wants Kalyla and Zarie to get along. I don't even see what's the big deal with that one. Shit, maybe I should have told Kalyla why I really was going to the restaurant, and maybe she would have been down to help a nigga out.

"Aye, what's good, my boy?" Zobie greeted, walking into my apartment.

"Ain't shit. Where you coming from, nigga?" I asked, slapping hands with my nigga.

"From Kalyla's spot," he announced like it was nothing.

"Why you went there? Y'all got something going on?" I interrogated.

"Nah, shorty is too hung up on you to notice anyone else," he replied.

"Man, take yo ass on with that shit. You know damn well I don't see her in that light. Nigga, you out of all people know damn well I don't have those type of feelings. Shit, you would be the first to know," I admitted.

I don't care what everyone else believes. The only reason why Kalyla and I are this way is because we were always together growing up. If you saw one, you saw the other, and I was cool with that. It's just everyone around us doesn't see it the same way. They see something totally different from how I feel. I can't say Kalyla was on the same page as me, but I hope like hell she was because that would ruin the friendship that we had.

"I don't think she's on the same page as you. You should really talk to her. I get that y'all are close, but there ain't no way she doesn't have stronger feelings for you. Every girl you've tried to get with she had a problem with and maybe that was okay since you were never really into all any of those other girls. You just wanted to fuck, so

Kalyla became your escape to having to be with someone. Now, you got shorty that you're interested in, and Kalyla is standing in the way."

"Nah that's not possible. She can't have feelings for me. Kalyla would have been said something. Y'all want her to have feelings for me so bad. Just because she's my best friend doesn't mean we have to end up together."

"You can try to convince yourself otherwise, but I think she does," Zobie replied.

"Man let's not talk about Kalyla. I need help planning something."

"Well, you're looking at the wrong nigga. I'm not no party planner. The fuck I look like, nigga?" Zobie murmured, kicking his feet up.

"Nigga, nobody said ya slow ass was a party planner. I just need some ideas so that I can get on Zarie's good side again."

"Nigga, you really like shorty like that? Nigga, you are doing a lot for a shorty that doesn't want to deal with you!" He pointed out.

"Yeah, and that's because I keep trying to push Kalyla on her. Kalyla won't be invited to this dinner party that I want to throw her with the fam," I confessed.

"Damn, you serious?"

"Yeah, I'm feeling shorty, and if Kalyla is really the problem, then I have to keep the two separate," I admitted.

"Well, damn. Do you, my nigga. It's about time your ass drew a line between you and Kalyla."

"Whatever I'm about to call my moms to see what she can come up with and go from there. Shit, I really need to figure out a way to get her to meet up with me. Zarie was really pissed, so I don't know if she will just show up because I ask her to."

"Nigga, you have to use that big ass head of yours. If SJ and her sister are still together, use the two of them. That shit will work out," he said, patting my shoulder.

"So Saturday you better be there."

"Ah nah, I don't know if I can make it. I know if you have that party and Kalyla won't be invited, she will definitely be calling me to hang out with her. So that's what I'll most likely be doing. Keep me updated on everything though."

"Yo, you like Lyla? What's going on there?"

"I've always been into her, but she ain't checking for a nigga like me. So, we cool being friends." He shrugged.

I made a mental note to bring that up to Kalyla. Zobie is a good nigga, so I don't know why she wouldn't want to be with that nigga.

****

Saturday was here, and a nigga was nervous as fuck. My Annie and my moms came through with putting my idea together. SJ said that Riah got Zarie to agree and come, so now it was just us waiting. Yeah, her birthday was almost two weeks ago, but it's the thought that count. Right now, I was low key regretting throwing this whole thing at my place because Kalyla was right down the hall, but shit, that was something I would have to deal with on another day. My whole apartment was decorated in black, gold, and silver.

I had the big ass balloons floating around the room. I even went as far as hiring a mixologist shorty that I'm always seeing all over Instagram. The family was over excited about meeting Zarie in person. On the other end, I was nervous as fuck. Zarie ass is a little cutthroat with the shit she be saying out her mouth.

"Aye, Riah said they're on their way up. She sent me a picture of how Zarie is dressed. Do you want to see what she has on?" SJ asked, scrolling through his phone.

"Nah, she on her way up here right? She is not pissed, is she?" I asked.

"Nigga, she doesn't know she's coming to your place. She thinks she's just come with Riah to meet the rest of the fam," he admitted.

"Why the hell y'all tell her ass that? Riah knows damn well her sister doesn't have a filter. If she comes in here flipping, I fuckin' both of y'all up," I gritted.

"Nigga, you fucked up, not us. So, you better hope her ass forgives you." SJ laughed as he made his way to the door.

When SJ opened the door, I was shocked as fuck to see DiZarie standing there in a form fitted black and nude dress that clung to her curvy figure. The dress stopped at the middle of her thigh, and she even had on heels. She even had her hair all nice and done up. This whole thing said a lot because shorty has mentioned it plenty of times on FaceTime that she hated getting her hair done. She only mentioned it so much because I always joked about her curly hair being all over the place. Zarie had a whole bunch of hair that's long and thick as fuck. With her hair in the natural state, it came down way past the middle of her back.

Anyway, back to right now. She looked good as fuck. Whatever lie they told her ass about tonight had to be a good ass one. Her coming along with Riah to a dinner to meet the fam wouldn't get her to dress like this.

"Oh hell no!" DiZarie called out and walked back out of my apartment.

"Hold on. I promise I'll get her to come back inside," Riah called out before rushing out behind her sister.

It took them a good fifteen minutes to come back, and the attitude was evident in DiZarie's face. I walked across the room to her, and she just gave me an icy look.

"Man, forgive a nigga. I fucked up not remembering your birthday but I'm trying to make it up now," I said, waving my hand around the room.

"Kalen, the effort is appreciated, but you could have just wished me a happy birthday and moved on."

"That's not how it works. I'm already invested into us," I replied.

"You can't do that, Kalen. Why did you have to get them to lie? I'm the only one here that's all dressed up. I look stupid. Oh, and who are all these people?" she gritted, pulling at the bottom of her dress.

"This is my family. I didn't know who else to invite." I shrugged.

"I'm not comfortable right now. Everyone else is wearing jeans and t-shirts while in a dress and heels. I am not staying here dressed like this."

I grabbed her hand and dragged her back to my room. If she didn't want to wear that, then I'll give her something to put on. We went into my room, and I cut the lights on. Walking over to my closet,

I watch as she kicked her shoes off and walked around my room touching shit.

"You can wear this," I called out giving her a pair of joggers, socks, and a wife beater.

"Kalen, they are going to look at me like I'm crazy," she groaned, looking at the clothing items in her arms.

"Just put it on. I'll make everybody leave if you want. I just tried to do something so that you won't be mad at me anymore."

"Why shouldn't I be mad at you anymore, Kalen? Are you inviting your girlfriend to this shindig?" She said, rolling her eye.

"Yeah, she just showed up. Now change and I'll be out there waiting for you," I said before leaving out the room.

"What's wrong with her? Her ass ain't speak to anyone or nothing," my Annie snapped as soon as I walked to the living room.

"She didn't feel comfortable with what she had on, so she's changing. SJ and Riah had her thinking it was some fancy dinner. Shorty doesn't normally dress like that, so I understand." I shrugged.

"Yeah okay," my Annie said, rolling her eyes.

Lord, that's not a good thing. Hopefully, when she came out, Zarie was in a better mood.

"Kalen!" I heard from behind me.

I turned scanning the room and saw Zarie standing over in the hallway looking scared as fuck. I went over to her and tried to pull her out into the living room where everyone else was.

"Wait!" She freaked, pulling me close to her. She was dead ass nervous right now.

"Are you serious right now? They want to meet you, and we are here to party. Have some fun," I said, wrapping my arms around her waist.

"I'm about to go out there with this on, and by the way, you are so small. There is no way we should wear the same size. Anyway, I don't know why you thought this would be a good time to meet the family," she whispered.

We both were standing in the hallway holding on to each other as I tried to convince her ass to come out.

"I met your family, so you will meet mine."

She stood in front of me pouting, but she wasn't getting out of this.

"It's not going to be bad," I assured her before going in for the kill.

I felt this was a good time. Without hesitation, I placed my lips on her, and she froze for a minute. However, her hesitation turned into her engaging in the kiss. Her arms wrapped around my neck and this shit felt like nothing I've ever experienced. I broke away from her, and I stared at her.

"If y'all were going to fuck, you could have told us not to come!" My Annie called out.

I turned around only to see everyone in attendance staring at us in the corner.

"Kalen!" DiZarie groaned, hiding behind me.

"Now you definitely have to meet the fam." I laughed, grabbing her hand and pulling her into the living room.

The first person I went to was my Annie. No matter the situation, she will always tell me the truth. Her ass has not one filter, and I love her for it.

"Annie!" I called out, getting her attention.

She turned around and instantly her arms were folded across her chest while she grilled the fuck out of Zarie.

"Annie, this is my girlfriend DiZarie. DiZarie, this is my Annie Nyrae."

"Hi, it's nice to meet you," DiZarie said shyly sticking her hand out.

"Hello! What are your intentions with my nephew?" my Annie fired off.

"Um, I'm not sure. I just learned we're in a relationship," Zarie shot back.

"So what are you trying to say? You're saying you too good for my nephew?"

"That's not what I am saying at all. What I am saying is that Kalen and I aren't together, but he loves to introduce me as his girlfriend. I like him, but I don't know. He has a complicated situation going on," Zarie explained.

"I do not see Kalyla like that, so you need to stop."

"Tell me anything," Zarie replied rolling her eyes.

"If you're not his girlfriend why were the two of you kissing just now?" Annie asked.

"I um… I don't know. I like him. I won't lie about that, but what I won't do is fight for a spot that's supposed to be mine, if he's doing all of this," Zarie shot back.

I was definitely enjoying the back and forth. The whole act she just did in the hallway was out the window.

"Do you want to be with him?"

DiZarie glanced over in my direction before playfully rolling her eyes and letting out a sigh.

"I can see myself being with him," Zarie admitted.

"Hell yeah, you can," I let out wrapping my around her and kissing the side of her face hard as hell.

"Ugh, Kalen, stop," Zarie let out laughing.

"I guess I approve of you. You hurt my nephew, and I hurt you," my Annie threatened before walking away.

By the look on Zarie's face, I could tell she was unfazed by the threat, and that shit turned me on. I grabbed her hand and went over to where my moms, pops, and Camille were standing so that I can introduce them to her.

"Aye, y'all listen up. It's time for introductions," I said as I walked up on their circle.

"Who's this beautiful girl?" My pops asked as he stuck his hand out.

"Hi my name is, DiZarie," she replied sticking her hand out.

"My girlfriend," I added.

"Ah, there is no need to be shy. You dating this knucklehead?" My father joked and pulled DiZarie into a hug.

"Um, I guess it just started since he's telling everyone that." DiZarie laughed.

"Well just be good to my son is all I ask," my moms said, hugging her.

By the look on Camille's face, I could tell that she wasn't happy about DiZarie. Camille was one of the people that wanted me and Kalyla to get together. They weren't about to force me into a relationship with Kalyla. I cherished our friendship so much more that I would never look at her in that way.

"Why isn't Kalyla here?" Camille questioned still giving DiZarie nasty looks.

"The two of them really don't get along, so today is about celebrating her birthday," I explained.

"Wow, you threw my daughter to the side for someone else you've known for how long?" Camille asked, sizing DiZarie up.

"I mean Lyla will always be my best friend. That's never going to change, but you and everyone else knows how territorial she is over me. She will ruin this whole thing before I ever get a good start with DiZarie." I laughed.

"Well, maybe this DiZarie girl is the problem and not my daughter. You threw away fifteen years of friendship for some ass. I thought you were better than that, Kalen."

"Excuse me?" Zarie snapped.

"Baby girl, nothing good comes to a woman that likes to cause havoc in other people's lives," Camille murmured.

"Did you ever think that maybe just maybe he didn't want your daughter? I've given him plenty of chances to walk away and work on whatever he had going on with shorty, and each time he declined. I'm trying to respect my elders, but please stop trying me. I'm not forcing him to do anything. All I asked is that he kept the two of us separated. Your daughter doesn't care for me, and the feeling is mutual. Anyway, it was nice to meet you all," Zarie said before walking off.

"Ma! What was that?" I asked.

"You know I want you and Kalyla to be together. That was always supposed to happen." She shrugged.

"But I don't have those type of feelings for her, and I don't even know how many times I have to tell everyone that. Kalyla doesn't like me in that way either. Y'all can't dictate our lives. Soon, she is going to have a nigga of her own, and all will be good," I assured.

"Well, I'm going to get out of here," Camille said before walking off.

What the hell was going on with everyone? They normally brought it up every once in a while, but shit, they were going hard with it. Then it's like they decided once I'm trying to get serious with someone that they want to constantly bring her up or insinuate that Lyla and I were something more than just friends. Kalyla and I will definitely have to have a sit down soon and make sure we that were on the same page.

DiZarie

The get-together Kalen threw for my birthday was unexpected but appreciated. I didn't like the fact that Kalyla's moms tried to come at me because Kalen didn't want to be with her daughter, but it did have me thinking. Was Kalen telling me he didn't see Kalyla like that but was really fuckin' with her while I wasn't around? I don't know, but once I feel like Kalen is on some fuck shit, I'm out of here. He wasn't about to have me out here looking crazy.

"Ugh, everybody's gone," Kalen groaned plopping down on the couch next to me.

Riah left with SJ, and I made her ass promise to call me once she walked through the door. Between her and Kalen, they were not trying to hear that I was leaving here tonight. I don't know what Kalen thought was about to happen, but he did have another thing coming. I have a little buzz going on, but I wasn't drunk right now.

"Did you enjoy yourself?" Kalen questioned, pulling my body close to his.

Getting comfortable, I placed my legs across his lap and nodded my head in agreement. Outside of the introductions and the situation with Kalyla's moms, the party was fun. They didn't make me feel unwelcome, and it was like I was partying with my people with the old school music blasting through the speakers and the adults dancing and drinking. His family really gave me a good vibe.

"So you still want to cut a nigga off?" he asked, rubbing his fingers through my hair.

"I really should still cut you off. I wasn't expecting this, so I guess this makes up for you not remembering I told you which day my birthday was," I replied.

"Oh, here," he voiced, reaching into his pocket.

He pulled out a blue Tiffany box, and I cut my eyes at him.

"No! I can't accept that. Besides the party was enough," I said, pushing the box away.

"Take the box," he demanded, shoving it into my hands.

I stared at him for a minute then decided to open the box and see what he got.

"Aww!" I cooed as I stared at the cute and thoughtful charm bracelet inside.

"You like it?" he asked, staring at the box.

"I love it," I cooed as I handed him the box so that he can put it on.

"I want to let you know that ain't shit going on with Kalyla and me. I don't see her in that light, and I don't know why these niggas acting like this is my first time telling their asses that."

"So is that what it's going to be like between us. I'm hanging out with you, and everyone brings up how you and ole girl belong together?" I asked.

"I don't know. I hope not, but I can't control what other mothafuckas have to say." He shrugged.

"Why haven't you two gotten together?"

"Because that's like having sex with my sister, and that shit will never happen," he admitted.

"Okay." I shrugged.

"Don't do that!" he chastised.

"I didn't say anything." I laughed.

"Whatever, what do you have to do tomorrow? Can you chill with a nigga?"

"I have a test to do some time tomorrow, and I don't know. I'll probably go to the mall or something. Why?"

"You not trying to chill with a nigga. Listen, we're together now, and you agreed to that shit. So that means our shit is official, and we need to spend time together and get to know each other more."

"I have a life outside of being your girlfriend, Kalen. My life doesn't stop because we are together. I am a woman that is about her business. I have goals to accomplish and I—"

"Aht, go on with all that shit. I know that, and it's what attracts me to you. However, I don't want to have to track your ass down to get you to meet up with a nigga. I know how your ass loves to go ghost. Is there time in your world for me?"

"Eh! I don't know. It depends. Kalen, if you expect me to be with you all the time, it isn't going to work," I said.

"I am not expecting all the time, but I do expect some of your time. So, after you do your test and I finish my training, are you going to chill with me?" he asked.

"Well, I guess I can," was all I got out when I heard his front door opening.

I turned some to see Kalyla and that Zobie guy walking in. I cut my eyes at Kalen and sucked my teeth. This cannot be happening right now.

"So I heard you had a party for this girl and I didn't even get... Oh, she's still here." Kalyla said as she entered, and I didn't miss the fact that her ass rolled her eyes at me either.

"Damn Camille ran down the hall to tell you that she was over here? You know ya moms was tripping tonight, don't you?" Kalen laughed.

"Yeah, everybody else is trippin' but you. How you doing, Desire?" Kalyla greeted.

"Shorty, move around because you know that's not my name," I said not even bothered to look in her direction.

"Damn, so what y'all do today?" Kalen asked his friends.

"How you doing, Ms. DiZarie?" his friend Zobie said.

"Heyy Zobie! How have you been?" I smiled.

Out of this whole little duo, he was the only one I was willing to be cool with. Fuck ole girl with her hating ass.

"I'm good. Mad I missed the party. Did you enjoy your time? Oh, and happy belated birthday," Zobie said.

"Thank you! Yes, I did enjoy my night. You should have come."

"Yeah, but I was chillin' with this knucklehead. The next party I'm definitely in there," he joked.

I just nodded my head and started looking through my phone. This whole thing right here was awkward as fuck, and shorty was who was throwing everything off. I needed to get the fuck up out of here. She was fuckin' up my energy.

"I'm about to go home," I announced, getting up from the couch.

"Why? We were just chillin' and talking," Kalen said, getting up as well.

"Why does she have my pants on?" Kalyla questioned.

"Are you serious?" I barked.

I pushed pass Kalen and stormed off to his room quickly getting out of the joggers I had on and snatched off the wife beater. I cannot believe this nigga would give me her fuckin' clothes to put on. What kind of shit is that? There I stood in my panties and bra pissed that we were having a good ass time and now this.

"Man, I really thought those were my pants," Kalen let out as he barged into his room.

There I stood in my underwear as Kalen lustfully stared at me. I normally would hate when anyone would objectify my body by the way he stared at me, but for the first time in forever, this gave me a different feeling.

"Umm," he let out shaking his head, but his eyes never my body.

"Can you get out? I'm trying to get dressed," I sassed.

"Damn, I didn't know you were stacked like that. How the hell do you hide all of this? Why don't you—"

"Nah, don't even. Get out so that I can get dressed. Also, my mind is way sexier. Get your life together!" I snapped.

"I get that your mind is sexy but damn."

I rolled my eyes and quickly put my dress back on. I didn't feel like wearing my heels, so I went into the closet to help myself to a pair of his slides. I'll give them back whenever I feel like it.

"So you just going to take my shit?" Kalen murmured.

I ignored him, slid my feet into his Burberry slides, and grabbed my bag to walk out of his room. When I passed through the living room towards the door, I saw Kalyla sitting there with a satisfied smirk on her face, and that did nothing but piss me off even more. I already had it in my head that I was about to curve the fuck outta Kalen, but oh nooo. This bitch was going to see me with this nigga all the time.

"Damn, Zarie! Wait, how are you going to get home?" Kalen inquired, grabbing my arm.

"Uber! I'll see you tomorrow." I cooed, wrapping my arms around his neck and kissing his lips.

I can hear Kalyla suck her teeth behind us and that warmed my soul. She can fight it all she wants, but I was going to have the last laugh. I was into this kiss way more than I planned. His tongue was exploring my mouth as I let out little moans. The feeling of his large hand groping my ass had me snapping out whatever kind of trance this nigga had me in. I need to shake Kalen because I'm getting too outside of my character. Never in life would I allow a nigga to objectify me like this, but rubbing this in Kalyla's face was more rewarding to me right now.

"Um, I'll see you tomorrow. Kyla and Zobie you two should do dinner with us tomorrow. I would love to get to know the two of you." I smirked before leaving out the door.

She wanted to play games with me, but her little world with Kalen was about to come crumbling down.

Kalyla

I don't even know why I brought my ass over to Kalen's place. A part of me was going to stay away, but after talking with my mother, I wanted my presence to be known. When I came here, it wasn't what I expected. It's weird as fuck to see Kalen all up on a girl he knows that I don't fuck with.

"Nigga, this shit isn't going to end well." Zobie laughed.

Kalen turned around with a goofy ass grin on his face looking like he was really falling for that bitch.

"What the fuck you talking about, nigga?" Kalen asked, plopping down on the couch.

"How is this going to play out? You two act like y'all can't survive being around each other. Then you have your girl who is obviously staking her claim and at the same time showing her obvious dislike for your best friend," Zobie pointed out.

"What? No, she is not! Kalyla started that shit man. I thought you said you were going to chill out," Kalen said, flipping it on me.

"Wow! What did I do wrong? She's the one with a problem and her kissing you like that wasn't necessary. At the end of the day, she can't compete," I concluded, rolling my eyes.

"There is no competition at all! She's my girl, and you're my best friend. You know that right?" he asked as he stared me down.

"What?"

"You don't have those kind of feelings for me, right? That's something that will NEVER happen. You know that, right?" Kalen said.

"Um, did I say that?" I didn't know what else to say.

I don't know, but since this girl done came into the picture, I didn't look at Kalen the same. I've always had Kalen to myself. I used to think that there wasn't a girl that could replace me in this world. Since this girl popped up, he stopped sleeping at my place. He was always texting or FaceTiming her. Then this shit right here. This nigga was really switching up on me.

"We on the same page, right? It's like once I want to get serious with someone, everyone is switching up. You moving funny and ya moms is talking crazy. Does she know something I don't know?"

"What would she know that you wouldn't know, Kalen?" I sassed, rolling my eyes.

"Shit, I don't know. I just want to make sure ain't nothing change between us. Everyone has been making it seem like one of us had a change of heart. I know it wasn't on my end," Kalen murmured.

"I don't know what everyone is talking about. My feelings have changed, but…"

"Kalyla, noo!" Kalen groaned.

"My feelings have changed about Zobie!" I lied.

I wasn't about to tell this nigga I was having mixed feelings about him so that he could play my ass.

"Aye, my nigga! Y'all together?" Kalen asked excitedly.

It was honestly pissing me off that he was reacting this way. Why wasn't he jealous? Shit, why have my feelings changed for Kalen? I'm all fucked up in the game right now.

"This is new to me." Zobie shrugged.

"Well, we are going to leave. Let Desire know we probably can make dinner. I don't know. We might want to chill in and fuck on each other. You know how the new couples get." I laughed as I stood up.

"Y'all leaving?" Kalen asked.

"Yeah, we are going to get out of here."

"Aight. Don't forget tomorrow we are going out. I want y'all two to get along."

"I'll let you know," I said rushing out the door with Zobie right behind me.

I wasn't going to dinner with him and that damn girl. What the fuck do I look like having a meal with that bitch. I need to figure out how to get rid of her. She fuckin' up everything around us.

"Why you lied to that man?" Zobie asked as we walked down the hall.

"How do you know my feelings for you haven't changed?" I challenged.

"Because I know you're in love with Kalen. I'll play along though," Zobie said, stopping at the elevator.

"You're not coming to my place?" I cooed.

"Nah. I'm going to head home. I have to work anyway," he said, getting on the elevator.

My life is a fuckin' mess right now.

****

"I talked with P. Storm, and he's down with letting Zobie join the team," Kalen informed me.

"Wait. What? I didn't know Zobie wanted to do this?"

"Yeah, that nigga doesn't like his current job, so I mentioned this to him. Shit, it's way more money than what he's getting now, and I'll have a partner since you don't want to do hits." He shrugged.

I just shrugged my shoulders in response. It was true I had no plan to do hits, so I guess it was cool.

"Yo, you sure you don't want to drive together? Zarie is going to meet us at the restaurant so she won't be in the car," he offered.

"Um, sure. Just know that you better take up for me when your girl starts her shit." I laughed.

"Man, she's trying, so I hope you will try too Kalyla. I'm really feeling shorty, and you know that never happens, so it should say a lot. Just try to get to know her for me," he pleaded.

"Fine Kalen," I replied.

I told his ass fine, but it was anything but fine. I will play for now but them staying in a relationship wasn't going to last. She had too much power over Kalen, and it happened too fast. There is no reason for her ass to be calling shots right now.

DiZarie is messing up everything in our lives right now. With her being around it's like Kalen doesn't care about me anymore. For fourteen plus years, it's always been Kalen and me against everyone. Now that she's in the picture it's like I don't even matter to him anymore. Yesterday when he announced that he didn't have feelings for me, it had me feeling some type of way.

****

I cannot believe he talked me into actually coming to this dinner. His little bitch showed up, and she was showing the fuck out.

The bitch came dressed in a pair of tight ass pants that showed all her curves. It pissed me off how Kalen and even fuckin' Zobie was drooling over her.

"So, how was your day? What test did you have to take?" Kalen questioned the little bitch.

"Hard as fuck. I don't know what the hell I was thinking of majoring in Biochemistry," she groaned.

"Wait! You dead ass going to school for that? The fuck you trying to do for a career?" Zobie inquired.

I sat back in my seat rolling my eyes because this bitch life was not that exciting.

"I want to be a forensic scientist. I've always found jobs like that interesting."

"Shorty, you serious right now?" Kalen cut in.

"Yeah! This is my last year. I'm on my last few classes and will be graduating next May," she crooned.

While these two niggas are fawning over this bitch, I wasn't impressed at all. Fuck her and her bitch ass degree.

"Damn, that's what's up! You better invite me to graduation too," Kalen said, pulling at her hair.

"Nigga you and my hair. Move!" She laughed, swatting his hand.

"That's a nice weave, who did that? You can barely see the lace," I pointed out.

"You haven't said anything to me since we got here and that's the first thing you say? You don't see a lace because this isn't a weave. It's all mine, baby girl. I don't need it!" the lil bitch snapped.

"Man, come on Zarie! She ain't mean it like that," Kalen defended.

Yes, about time he put that bitch in her place. I was trying to be funny but still!

"Whatever, Kalen. Ole girl is a hater, but I guess I would hate on me too," the bitch had the nerve to say.

"I know this bitch didn't say I was hating on her!" I snapped.

"Call me out of my name again and watch what happens. If you have a problem with me being with your nigga just say that. Bitch, you will get more respect from me being honest. I'll probably even consider leaving your nigga alone so that you can try to claim the spot you so desperately want. But this little girl shit you're doing is pissing me off, and I'm honestly trying to refrain from putting my hands on ya hoe ass," the lil bitch gritted.

"Whoa! Baby, nah, that's not about to happen," Kalen defended.

"You can't tell me what's about to happen. Shit honestly, I don't even know why I'm doing this shit with her ass. I don't fuckin' like her, and I'm not about to have her ass acting funny because her ass wants to fuck you. It's not my fault the two of y'all haven't fucked yet," she argued.

"Bitch, who said I wanted to fuck him? You don't know shit, so you don't need to speak on shit. I will continue to do what the fuck I want, and you ain't stopping shit!" I spat.

"Hmp. You don't know me too well. Just because I know my worth and I'd rather have my face in a book doesn't mean shit. I will rag tag yo ass and not give a fuck what anyone thinks about it. Kalen maybe your *best friend*, but that doesn't mean shit to me!" she spat.

"Man, DiZarie, I'm not about to let you put hands on her. Both of you are taking it too far. All this shit is for no reason at all. You're my girl, and Kalyla is my best friend. Besides her ass has feelings for Zobie. She don't want a nigga like that. You trippin'," Kalen voiced.

"If you can't see shorty wants you, then I'm just going to say that you don't want to see it. It's fuckin' obvious to everyone around you. Nigga, I know someone taught her ass to go by a person's actions and not want they say. This bitch's action is saying *I wish I were riding my best friend!*" DiZarie spat.

"Oh shit," Zobie let out laughing.

"Man," Kalen started to say.

"Nahhh! Listen, I was honestly going to give this a try. I am feeling you no lie, but her I am not willing to deal with. I'm not with all this, so I'm about to get out of here. Thanks for the party and thank you for trying to get to know me, but I'm good on all of this," she announced, getting up from the table.

"Man, Zarie! Wait, what the fuck just happened?" Kalen called out, rushing behind her.

"You keep it up, and that nigga is really gonna start limiting his time around you. He obviously likes ole girl. You see how that nigga just chased her ass out of here? Let it had been anyone else, and he wouldn't have gave not one fuck. You need to tell that nigga you want to be with him or leave that damn girl alone," Zobie schooled.

"I don't want him like that, and I don't think he should be with her either. Kalen can be with anyone else. So stop being dramatic, Zobie!" I groaned.

He just shook his head and laughed. I didn't see anything funny, and I also stand by what I believe. Kalen should not be with that girl.

Kalen

Damn dinner the other day did not go how I thought it would. Here I am thinking that Kalyla would have tried to be nice to my girl, but she was picking. Then I have DiZarie going off on her ass not making shit any better. I tried to cut that shit, but both of them weren't letting up at all. It's been three days since that shit happened, and DiZarie really wasn't fuckin' with a nigga. Since that shit went down, I've been keeping my distance from Kalyla too. She can try to act like she doesn't know why a nigga was creating distance if she wants, but I know I had a talk with her ass before that dinner, and she told me that she would chill the fuck out.

There was no part of that dinner where she chilled the fuck out. She told me that she would give her a try. That dinner was not her trying at all. Now back to the present. I was sitting waiting to see if Zarie would reply to any of my text messages. My ass should be in my grandpops house for this meeting, but I wanted to see if she was going to respond. I sent her five messages within the last twenty minutes, and it was pissing me off that I had to try this fuckin' hard to get in contact with her ass. I read over my last few texts to her and shook my head.

Me: *You dead ass going to ignore a nigga.*

Me: *We not going to talk this shit out?*

Me: *You spit all that shit at the dinner and then dip out.*

Me: *You are really pissing a nigga off. Don't be mad when I pop up on that ass.*

Me: *I see you think I'm joking. I don't hear from you in the next hour I'm pulling up on your ass.*

Damn, I see she don't think a nigga will pull up on her ass. After this meeting with P. Storm, I was definitely going to look for her ass. I needed a little help though. Of course, my little cousin was about to get his girl to help me out because I see they are my only help when it comes to her ass.

Me: *SJ I need help a little. Find out where the hell DiZarie is and how long she will be there. I need to know her whereabouts for the rest of the day because I have to pull up on her ass.*

My phone chimed showing that nigga didn't waste no time getting back to me. When I checked the message, I saw it wasn't even SJ hitting a nigga back. It was DiZarie.

Zarie: *I'm not responding to your messages for a reason. I know I was perfectly clear when I told you that I didn't want anything to do with you. I don't have time to sit there and argue with another female about something so damn stupid. THAT IS NOT THE TYPE OF WOMAN THAT I AM! It's like when I'm around you, I don't act the way I'm supposed to. If you want to be friends cool, but if you want anything else, I'm good on you. I really suggest you work out whatever you have going on with your so-called best friend before going to be in a relationship with someone else. Oh, and please stop saying y'all don't feel that way for each other. You may not, but she does. No one that didn't have feelings for someone would behave this way. I never gave that girl a reason to come at me the way she does. That tells me and EVERYONE AROUND YOU that she wants more than your friendship. Please stop contacting me.*

I reread her message again and again before stuffing the phone into my pocket. There was no way in hell she was about to tell me what was going on between Kalyla and I. At this point in life, I don't give a fuck how she feels about me. What matter is the fact that I don't want her ass that way! No matter how many times or how many different languages I had to say that shit in, I do not want her ass. I saw her as nothing but a sister! Not all best friends fall in love with each other. Man, I definitely meant what I said when I texted SJ I was going to pull up on her ass. There was no way in hell it was about to end at that bullshit ass message.

I got out of my truck and made my way inside of my grandfather's home. I already knew everyone was probably waiting for me in his office, and I was going to hear some slick shit before we even got started with the meeting. Just like I knew it would all eyes was on me when I entered the office.

"It's nice of you to join us. I said three thirty for a reason, Kalen," P. Storm chastised.

"Okay, I had to handle some shit. I was outside on time though," I disputed as I went around the room greeting everyone and making sure to skip Camille along with Kalyla's ass.

"Ew, what's wrong with you?" Camille questioned.

"Can we get the meeting started? I have some other things to get it," I announced ignoring her question.

"Kalen is upset because his little bitch doesn't want anything to do with him." Kalyla laughed.

"Oh, so you think that shit is funny. It's all because you won't hop off my dick!" I snapped.

"Whoa now!" P. Storm called out holding his hands up.

"Nah, there was never a time where I was all in her business and fuckin' blocking her shit like she is doing right now. That shit is crazy, even after I fuckin' talked to her ass about and she fuckin' told me that she was going to chill out. That girl ain't do a gah damn this to Kalyla's hateful ass. That shit crazy but maybe I need to start listening to what everyone been saying! You must really want a nigga," I ranted.

"I do not want you Kalen so calm down," she sassed.

"Then hop off my shit. Why the fuck are you so pressed about who the fuck I want to be with? You should be cool with that shit as my best friend. You step in if you see she's doing some fucked up shit towards a nigga. You are just doing that shit for your own personal reasons, even when I told your ass that I didn't see your ass like that. I do not see you in a sexual way! You are like the sister I never had. I've said this many times. Let that shit register in your damn head! Can we get to the meeting so that I can go on about the mothafuckin' business?" I gritted.

Everyone in the office sat there shocked that I went the fuck off like that, and Kalyla was looking stupid in the face. Good! I don't ask her ass for much, and this one thing I asked her to do, her ass couldn't even do.

"What the fuck is so special about this bitch? Why the fuck are you coming so hard at me over this one bitch? There are many times I've done shit like this and not once did you act like this!" Kalyla snapped.

"That right there should fuckin' tell you something. I'm popping up at dinners. I went to the fuckin' zoo with her ass. I am either on the phone or texting with her ass all day nonstop. I'm fuckin' feeling her, and I've told you this. I told you this, and it's like you don't give a fuck. There was never a time I went hard like this behind no girl, and you don't even give a fuck about that. Before that mothafuckin' dinner, we talked about it, and you told me you understood, yet as soon as shorty sat her ass in the seat you started up."

"You didn't even defend me when she started coming at me," she accused.

"Hell nah, you can't even say that! I tried to stop that shit, and you kept baiting her ass. What the fuck is so hard with you being cordial with her. You don't like her cool but respect her enough because of me. You got ya moms gassing your head, and you need to stop it. Camille, you too fuckin' old to be in our business anyway because—"

"Hell nah! Watch your mouth, Kalen. Don't disrespect her. You may not like what she's doing or how she handled your little girlfriend, but you will respect your elders!" My pops snapped.

"So everyone is going to come at me because of the shit they're doing? When is someone going to check them for it? I sit there and brag about how dope my family is and two major people in my life are walking around doing all this. That shit was fuckin' crazy! Can we do this meeting? I got some things to do?" I snapped.

"Kalen," Camille called out.

"Please don't say anything to me right now. I just want to get this meeting so that I can go about my business," I announced.

"Damn, the little nigga is pissed! Well, this shit was so we can discuss what the hell y'all going to do. Is it jobs or are y'all starting businesses? You have ya friend joining in, so I already know your answer is to continue training. It's really Kalyla who I need the answer on," P. Storm announced.

"Who would be my partner if Zobie and Kalen pair up?" She asked looking over in my direction.

"The twins are getting older, and I know SJ talked his parents into letting him start earlier, so if push comes to shove, it would be him."

"Ummm, I think I'm going to go with the business. I'm not trying to be out there like that. I will finish the training if I have to though," Kalyla announced.

"Aight well, I see that shit between the two of y'all are really tense. Kalen, I know you mad now but remember at the end of the day, they're family," P. Storm exclaimed.

"Nah! I get their family, but that doesn't mean I have to sit here and be around them all the time. Oh, and you need to be telling them that. I'm good over here. I haven't don't anything wrong to either one of them," I replied.

"Aight little nigga. I see shit ain't going to register to you right now, and I'm not going to keep repeating myself. You can leave. Continue with training and make sure your friend is all in too. Bring him by too so that he and I can talk to him about money. I know he quit his other job for this, and I'm not about to have him out here with his pockets on E until he gets his first assignment," P. Storm stated.

"No doubt. I'll hit him up and probably be back here before the week ends. Or shit maybe she can bring him since she is all of a sudden feeling that nigga." I laughed sarcastically.

Everyone's eyes with to Kalyla and that was my cue to leave out. I checked my phone and saw that SJ hit me up with Zarie's moves. The little nigga is always coming through. I'm about to go pull up on her ass at school. It says her class ends in another thirty minutes. Yeah, she's about to see me.

****

I've been sitting here waiting for her ass to come out of the building. Her class ended a good ten minutes ago, and her ass still hasn't come out. She had a nigga out here looking like a fuckin' creep sitting on the hood of my car just watching people. I pulled my phone out and decided to call her ass and see where the fuck her ass was. The phone rang once before going straight to voicemail. She had a nigga blocked! DiZarie definitely knows how to get on a nigga's bad side. She wants me to curse her ass out.

Then here she comes strutting out the fuckin' building with no fuckin' books in her hands and smiling in another nigga's face. Why the fuck is she testing me right now? Here she is walking with this fuck nigga and barely has on clothes too. I mean her top could be covered better. Her ass didn't need to be showing any kind of skin if she got a nigga. Zarie had on this big ass pair of sweat pants that were rolled at the waist and barely hanging on. One of those stupid ass half of sweatshirts on showing her whole damn stomach. Yeah, she was really showing the fuck out.

"YEEERRRRRRR!" I shouted out with my hands cuffed around my mouth.

She stopped walking and automatically turned in my direction. I wasn't trying to show my ass right now, so I was about to pull my shit out like I wanted to. Zarie was going to try me, and I could tell from her stance alone. She saw me over here waiting for her ass, but yet she is still in that nigga's face.

"Aye! I know you heard my fuckin' yerrrr! The fuck you over there in another nigga's face? Let's go!" I demanded.

DiZarie still took her time with that nigga, and when she decided to hug him, it really pissed me off. She really didn't know she just fucked up. I watched as he took the bag off his back and headed it over to her then transferring the books in his hands to her. They shared a few more words before she stomped her way over to me.

"Kalen, did you no get my message? I don't want to see you!" She spat, slamming her big ass books on the hood of my truck.

"Man, don't disrespect my shit like that. Here I am coming to pick my girl up after her classes and you out here smiling hard as shit in another nigga's face. That's disrespectful as fuck, and if we weren't on this school campus, I would have probably shot at y'all asses!" I snapped.

"You wouldn't have to see me with someone else if your ass didn't show up here. I told you that I was good on you. Why would you pop up here?" She snapped.

"Because this ain't that kind of party. That shit you got going on with Kalyla is just that, some shit between the two of you. I can't force her to do right no matter how many times I asked her ass to chill out. You want too much from a nigga, shorty. As long as I'm still by your side and I don't allow another mothafucka to disrespect, that should be enough," I voiced.

"Are you truly explaining yourself to me? I don't care how you break it down. We don't need to go any further than this. At the end of the day, these people are your family, and I don't want to come in between that. We haven't been together for that long, so it doesn't matter," she reasoned.

Was she dead ass right now? How in the fuck could she not see that a nigga was feeling the fuck out of her? Her ass was so damn stuck on what the fuck Kalyla might feel about me knowing damn well I didn't feel the same no matter how many times I said that shit to her ass and to everyone around us. Maybe she's right though. A nigga was stuck on stupid when it came to her ass, and I couldn't even explain that shit myself. Yeah, a nigga needed to walk away from her hot and cold ass.

"Aight bet you got it," I exclaimed, getting off the hood of my car.

I went over to the driver side of the door and climbed then shut the door behind me. She stood in the same place looking at me in the front view of the car mirror, and I just cut the car on. Her ass probably didn't think a nigga was going to say fuck it. Since I met her ass, I've been chasing behind her ass. Nah, I wasn't about to do this shit again. DiZarie still stood there looking with her shit sitting on my car like a nigga wasn't ready to go.

"Aye, shorty, get that shit off my car because your shit will be on the ground!" I shouted out once my window was rolled all the way down.

"Nigga, are you serious right now?" She snapped.

"The fuck you mean am I serious? Didn't you just hear me say that shit out of my mouth? I am dead the fuck serious. Move yo shit Zarie so that I can go on about my business," I gritted.

"Nigga, you cannot be serious right fuckin' now!" She yelled.

She thought I was joking with her ass. I put the gear into reverse and started backing out of the space. Her mouth dropped open, and she ran towards the car.

"Yeah, I got her ass now," I said out loud to myself.

I slammed on the brakes to stop, and I was thinking I had her ass, but nah she got me. She dug into her pocket and stabbed something into my tire. I threw my gear into park and jumped out my car. As I made my way towards her, I saw her ass trying to get something out of my tire. Once I was over on her side, I saw her crazy ass trying to yank the damn knife she stuck into my tire out.

"The fuck you do that for?" I snapped, yanking the knife out the tire.

I closed up the knife before sliding it into my pocket. With my arms folded across my chest, I waited for her damn explanation.

"The fuck you do that for? You can't hear shit now?"

"Nigga, I heard what the fuck you said. I popped your tire because that was disrespectful as fuck to walk the fuck off while I'm talking to you. I know what the fuck I was saying to you, but nigga, respect me enough to not play in my face," she sassed.

"What the fuck I need to sit around and go back and forth with your ass? You said you didn't want to be bothered with a nigga, and I fuckin' get the picture. I've been chasing behind your ass since we fuckin' started this shit. What the fuck you want me to do now? I don't have control over different mothafuckas. I can't control how they see you, and I can't control what the fuck they say to you. I guess Kalyla was right." I shrugged.

"The fuck you mean she was right?"

"She said you ain't the one for me. Other mothafuckas were getting the boot because they didn't get along with her. Here I am going all out and fighting with my best friend for you, and you don't give a fuck. How many times have I tried to tell you this one simple thing, but nooooo, you don't give a fuck and don't want anything to do with a nigga. Fine. I give in. You want to be done with a nigga then cool," I expressed.

"Whatever Kalen," she shuttered as she gathered her things from the hood of my car.

Fuck her. She wanted this shit, so I'm going to give it to her. I was tired of this shit being one-sided. I saw myself being with DiZarie because the shit to me could be so fuckin' dope between us, but she had to get over this Kalyla shit. This time I was going to let her come to her senses because now it was her time to choose that giving us a try was worth it. I can't keep trying to force her into this shit. I also can't make her see this shit how I see it.

DiZarie

I don't care how many times I've told myself that having no contact with Kalen was best for the both of us, but I knew the shit wasn't true. It hasn't even been that long since he said he was done chasing me, and I'm already acting like it's been years. I missed hearing my phone chime notifying me I got a text. Shit, I even missed his annoying ass FaceTiming me. Why did it feel like a drastic change?

"Zarie! Can you come with me to SJ's dad's house? They're having a cookout, and I didn't want to go by myself." Riah asked, bursting her way into my room.

"Damn, you can't knock on the door? I don't think that's a good idea for me to go," I declined.

"Whyyy? I really want to go, but I just don't want to feel uncomfortable," she pleaded.

"Riah, that's your boyfriend. You've met his family already." I replied.

"Okay but that's doesn't mean anything. I will still feel singled out. It's his whole family. Come on, Zarie," she begged.

"What time is the cookout? I need to finish up this homework before I leave to go anywhere," I caved.

"Okay cool. I'll go get ready, and you just let me know when you're ready to leave!" she exclaimed before squealing and running out my room.

I closed out the books that were spread all over my bed and put them up. I lied about the homework because I definitely finished like an hour ago. There was something I needed to do before I went around Kalen and his family. The top priority was to make sure I looked fucking good to ensure that I had his attention. I wasn't even going to ask my mother to fix my hair up because all I was going to get from her was an I told you so. She had told me I made a mistake breaking things off with Kalen, and at the time I wasn't trying to hear what she had to say. She was right though. I didn't think I would miss the conversations with him. I didn't think I cared that much about what happened between us. In a short amount of time, he was able to make some kind of impact on my life.

****

"Get out the car, Zarie. You look cute, so I don't know why are you so nervous?" Riah called out as she stood on the driver side of the door waiting for me to cut my car off and get out.

I don't know why I was so damn nervous right now. I looked out the window, and she stood outside with our bag strapped across her body waiting for me to get out. I should have declined. I didn't think all of this through. First off, I had on this damn jumper shorts on with the rips on them, and these shits barely covered my ass, but for the jumper, I had the front and the straps hanging down. All I had on underneath was my bathing suit and this see-through top. My feet adorned in a pair of cute buckle strapped sandals.

"DiZarie! Get out the car!" Riah snapped, bagging on the car window.

I quickly pulled down the visor to make sure my hair was all good. My little attempt to do something to my hair came out okay. The front middle section of my hair was slicked back and put into a top knot with the rest of my kinky curls hung free. Letting out a shaky breath, I got out my car, and I was ready to go in the back.

As we trotted towards the backyard of the house, I could hear the people laughing and the music blasting. The closer we got to the backyard, the sweatier the palms of hands got. Once we were fully in the backyard, it was like they had a silent indicator because damn near everyone turned around to watch us walk over to everyone.

"Riah, what's good baby?" SJ greeted, pulling her into a hug.

It was cute seeing my little sister happy in a relationship.

"Aye, you decided to come. What's up, DiZarie? Kalen is over there with Zobie and Kalyla," SJ informed me, pointing in their direction.

"Um, I'm good on that," I replied.

"Damn. I don't know what's going on with y'all. Y'all can go say wassup to my people, and I can take y'all to where the food is. Give me your bag. I can put that inside for y'all," SJ said, taking the bag from Riah and strapping it across his body.

Both Riah and I followed behind him as he went over to the group of adults.

"Ma!" SJ called out.

Two different women turned around to look at him. I thought that Nyrae lady was his mother.

"They just wanted to say wassup to y'all. I'm about to show them around and get them some food," he announced.

Everyone spoke to us, and we spoke back, but as soon as Riah and SJ walked off, I was stopped from leaving.

"Jana, this the girl I was telling you about. She's Kalen's girlfriend," Nyrae said, pulling on my arm taking me over to some light skin lady.

"Ohh, she's a pretty one too. How long are you going to last? Everyone knows Kalyla acts like a damn dog when it comes to Kalen. She is so damn territorial." The Jana lady laughed.

"Oh, we aren't together. So, it didn't last that long," I informed letting out a nervous chuckle.

"What you mean y'all aren't together? Did you two just start up?" Nyrae probed.

"Yeah, but I wasn't feeling it. It wasn't going to work out too good."

"Why do you say that?" She questioned.

"Because for one I don't like that Kalyla girl. I tried to you know extend an olive branch and invited her and Zobie out with Kalen and me. It turned out bad. So, for one I don't want to feel like I'm fighting for a spot that's supposed to be mine, and then I felt like I was causing problems. He would explain how close they are and her role in his life, but that didn't change how she felt about me. That doesn't change that it will be a problem every time the two of us were around each other. The only resolution would be him not being around her, and I'm not that type of person. I can't make him cut off someone that has been there for a good portion of his life." I voiced.

"Girl, never let another female run you from your man. Do you have feelings for my nephew?" Nyrae asked.

"Yes," I truthfully answered.

"Then go be with him. Don't let others around him dictate how you two go about y'all relationship," she schooled.

"I hate the catty nonsense. I hate arguing with other females because I get headaches. I'd rather throw hands. I feel like if I have to get to that point with shorty, I need to distance myself. That dinner made me want to drag her. She doesn't know me, but she keeps playing with me. I don't have time for it," I admitted

"Girl, if it comes to that, then beat her ass. Now I shouldn't be saying that because she's my niece, but I also don't do that whole playing in no one's face. I am a firm believer in beating a bitch's ass that plays with you. So, I will advise you to go get your man, and if push comes to shove, beat her ass," Nyrae advised.

I just laughed and shook my head. I understood what she was saying, but I wasn't about to go over there and try to rekindle something between us.

"Aye, what are you doing here?" I heard from behind me.

"Op! Kalen put a little umph in his voice." The Jana lady laughed walking off with Nyrae.

Turning around to face him, he stood there staring me down waiting for my response.

"I'm here with my sister. What am I not allowed here?" I sassed.

"Nah, I didn't say that. How you been? What's up with you?" He inquired, stepping closer to me.

I took a step back and glared at him.

"It's only been a good couple of days. I've been good. What's up with you?" I shot back.

"I'm good. You want to come over here with us?"

"Nah, I don't think that's a good idea," I declined.

"If she says something, I will shut it down. We don't have to be together. We can be friends," he suggested.

"Fine," I agreed.

He grabbed my hand, and we walked over to where they were sitting. Instantly Zobie stood to his feet to hug me after greeting me. Kalyla looked at me with her nose all turned up like she was disgusted by me. I walked right past her ass and took a seat in one of the chairs next to Kalen. The table was dead silent, and I know it was only because I was over here.

"I see you got the legs out. You showing the fuck out, huh?" Kalen laughed playfully slapping my thigh.

"Riah told me it was a swim thing. It's also hot as hell out here. But you know I was so uncomfortable once it sunk in that I was going to be around a lot of people." I laughed.

"I don't know why. You look fine to me. That ass too." He laughed.

"Kalen! Don't do that," I scolded.

He knew I didn't like when he did that.

"Aw, I'm joking but seriously if you know what I mean. I'll stop talking about your body. I see you combed your hair today," he joked, pulling at my curls.

"You are just a gah damn Kevin Hart today. You got jokes for days I see you," I sarcastically let out.

"Come on, Zarie. You already know a nigga is hilarious. Do you miss a nigga yet?" He questioned.

"I guess you can say that. It seems like everyone else I text is just so boring now," I said, pouting.

"See right there you just proved you're feeling a nigga. You're letting people get into your head and now look," he boasted.

"Oh please! Don't flatter yourself. I'm just shocked you're an actual cool person," I joked rolling my eyes.

"Whatever! So, you ready to give in or are we still going to act like or aren't feeling a nigga?" Kalen questioned.

"I never said I wasn't feeling you so don't do that. I just—"

"Ugh, so you're just going to act like you don't see me here?" Kalyla spat, cutting me off.

"What are you talking about?" Kalen questioned, giving him her attention.

I rolled my eyes and sat back in my seat. This bitch wanted attention so damn much that it was sickening.

"Listen, Desire. I am very over protected of Kalen because—"

"Don't even continue. You know my name isn't Desire. You can try to have a real conversation with me and still trying to be petty with it. I don't know you and if you want to keep that energy don't speak to me," I cut in shutting her ass down.

"Oh, excuse me, DiZarie. I don't know why your name is programmed like that in my head. I want to let you know that I will back up from y'all relationship. I don't want to be the reason why he isn't happy. I'm just overprotective of him because you never know with females. They see the life that we live, and they want to be a part of it."

"Wait! Do you know me? Do you know my family?" I inquired.

"What do you mean?" She snapped, sitting up in her seat.

"First off, I am not a broke bitch that needs a nigga for anything. My family has that covered. All of this isn't anything new to me. You off the rip had a problem with me because of him. Also, you won't admit the real reason behind it. We can agree to cut the catty bullshit. I actually like Kalen, so this is about to happen again. I just don't want to go through the shit with you every time we are around each other," I voiced.

"So you trying to be with a nigga? You didn't run that by me." Kalen laughed.

"Ugh, here we go. You want me to slash your other tires? You know Kalen you bring out a side of me that I don't like. I have stopped doing things like this. I'll admit I haven't gone to the extreme like this before but," I gritted, rolling my eyes.

"That's because you're really feeling a nigga. My Annie done shot at my unc a couple of times. That's how relationships work."

"Oh lord. You think that's normal? My mother and father aren't like that. I also pride myself in being level headed and—"

"Hell nah! You aren't level headed. You don't like having problems like the whole arguing and shit, but I do believe you have a crazy side, which is why my tire was sliced. I'm still trying to figure out where you get the knife from," Kalen said checking me out.

"Wouldn't you like to know. Oh, and don't try to act like you know me." I giggled.

"Okay, so I would like to finish what I've been trying to say to you," Kalyla cut in.

"Oh yeah sure, what's up?" I let out, giving her my attention.

"I know it will not happen overnight, but I am willing to you know to chill out and get to know you. Kalen is obsessed with you for some reason, and I don't want everything to change between us. So that means I have to accept you and be friends with you," she explained.

I didn't like her explanation, so I was definitely about to shut her down.

"Aye!! Look at Kalyla on her grown woman shit," Zobie hyped.

"It's a difference between us being cordial and being friends. We don't have to be friends to be in each other's space. I already got what I needed to know about you. I can be around you and not be rude, but I wouldn't be your friend. I respect you enough to not come at you all wrong, and I hope from now on you will respect me as his girl."

"You my girl again?" Kalen questioned.

"What are you saying I'm not?" I quizzed staring him down.

"Hell nah, I'm not saying that. I'm just saying you were trippin' before."

"Okay, we are talking about here and now. Yeah, I said what I said before, but now I feel differently," I murmured.

"So y'all cool. I can go out with my girl and invited my two best friends to come along? Y'all won't be out here throwing petty jabs at one another?" Kalen asked.

"Yeah, I'm good on this end. There won't be a problem from me," I vowed.

"Same here," Kalyla agreed.

Her mouth was saying she agreed, but the look in her eyes told me something different. I will always make sure I'm on defense when it came to Kalyla. But what his aunt said to me and how I've been feeling since not talking to him, I wasn't going to push a relationship with Kalen away from me anymore. I need to let that shit roll off my back and stick to what I want. Now at this moment, I can firmly state that I want a relationship with him, so I'll keep it positive, but I wasn't about to be her friend.

Kalen

Yeah! A nigga finally got DiZarie ass to act right. She was here and outright telling a nigga straight up what she wanted. I didn't have to force her ass into something, and the fact that she and Kalyla will be cordial to one another had a nigga on cloud nine right now. I just hoped that Kalyla stuck to what she was saying now because she said she would be nice before, and the dinner turned out to be a disaster. Now here we are all at the cookout and Kalyla is actually talking to Zarie. Zarie was a little closed off, but at least she was responding to her. Shit, that's all a nigga can ask for.

"Aye, you want some food? They have mad barbecue out here in the back, but they also have seafood being cooked on the inside too. My Annie ordered from some online place and had this special sauce made. I'm about to go get my pan and come back to this table to smash. That the sauce everyone's been making in those damn YouTube videos with those seafood boils."

"Kalen, what are you talking about?" Zarie cut in laughing.

"You don't watch those videos on YouTube of those people eating crab legs and shit like that. Kalyla is obsessed with those videos. It's one of the videos where you just watching other people eat food and shit. But all them videos always got this damn sauce in it, and my Annie got a chef to come and make that shit. So, I'm about to go grab a pan and smash," I informed.

"Okay! Yeah, I want some food. I don't know about the seafood though. I'm not trying to smell like seafood, but if your food looks good, I might want some," Zarie added.

"Hell nah! You already trying to pick over my food and shit. Come on," I announced, standing to my feet.

She stood to her feet and this shit felt like the first time I ever saw what she had on. DiZarie had a lot of hips and ass, so I'm confused on why she thought these shorts were okay.

"Whoa, I'm just taking a good look at your outfit. What the fuck is going on here?" I asked pulling at the bottom at her shorts.

"Don't do that. It's nice out, and I have my bathing suit on under here. I wasn't about to put some pants on over a bathing suit," she explained.

"Yeah, whatever. Come on and let's go get some food," I said, walking off.

I can hear her talking shit behind me as we walked towards the house. When we entered the kitchen, a lady was transferring the king crab legs from the pots to separate pans full of sauce, big ass shrimp that was almost the size of my hand, lobster tails, along with corn, sausage, and potatoes.

"That's a lot. Are you really going to eat all of that?" Zarie asked, staring at the aluminum pan that I grabbed off the counter.

"Hell yeah. I'm about to fuck up this whole pan. All of this smell good as fuck. That sauce better be hitting too," I murmured.

"Are you going to share with me? I want barbecue, but that right there looks good. Especially those shrimps."

"I don't know if I want to share, but come on so that you can get some food, and I can go buss down this pan."

We both walked back outside and made our way over to the table full of food. Once we were over there, Zarie grabbed a plate and went pan to pan loading food onto her plate.

"Shorty, are you going to eat all of that? Hell nah," I laughed.

She picked up a rib and took a bite before closing her eyes and moaning as she chewed her food. That moan that left her mouth had a nigga at full attention. My eyes instantly went to her lips, and she even chewed sexy.

"Let me taste," I ordered.

She held the rib she took a bite of to my lips. Once I took a bite, I knew what the fuck she was moaning about because that shit was hitting.

"Aye put some extra on your plate for me," I voiced.

"That's exactly why I have all this on my plate. See, look. I'm willing to share with you, and you want to be stingy. Is there anything else you want from this table?" she inquired, looking around at the different stuff on the table.

"Nah if I want something, I'll come back to get it. I need to eat," I expressed.

"Wait, what about this?" she asked, pointing at the pan of deviled eggs.

"Nah, I don't eat those," I declined.

She shrugged her shoulders and started making her way back over to the table. I walked behind her and watch her hips sway side to side, and the way her shorts hung on her hips had a nigga in a trance. Maybe I should be happy that she doesn't dress like this all the time because I would have to fuck these niggas up looking at her. When we got back to the table, Kalyla and Zobie were all in a conversation, but as soon as we sat down, all conversation stopped.

"Damn, what are y'all over here talking about?" I probed.

"Nothing. I'm about to get some food. Come on, Zobie," Kalyla commanded before walking off.

****

After eating and sitting on the side chilling, I wanted to get into the pool. So here I am jumping in the pool now trying to convince DiZarie to jump in.

"Come on shorty get in. What you not trying to get your hair wet?" I joked.

She stood at the edge of the pool in this purple and gold high waist tribal print bathing suit. *Damn, she looked good as fuck.*

"This water is cold. Why can't the water be a little warm? I hate cold pools," she whined.

"If I have to get out, I'm going to just push your ass in. Come on," I demanded.

She rolled her eyes as she sat down on the side and put her feet into the water. I saw over to her and splashed water on her. You would have thought a nigga threw acid on her ass with how dramatic she was acting right now.

"Ahhh! Why would you do that!" She freaked and got back up.

"Get ya ass in the pool! You took your clothes off so niggas can stare at your ass. Get in." I laughed.

She slowly sat down on the side and slipped her feet back into the pool.

"Are you going to get your hair wet? Take the ponytail out," I ordered, staring her down.

She gave me a side eye but still let her hair free and unraveled the little bun she had on her head. Once that was out, I grabbed her around her waist and fell back into the water taking her under with me.

"Ugh!! You are so damn childish. Why would you do that, Kalen?" Zarie whined, making her way towards the edge of the pool.

"Don't get out! You already in," I laughed.

I went to grab her and pulled her back to my body.

"This water is still cold. I can't believe you did this," she shrieked.

She was legit mad right now. I moved to stand in front of her and pulled her body close to mine. Pushing her hair out of her face she looked up at me and rolled her eyes.

"Why you always got an attitude, shorty?" I questioned.

"I don't always have an attitude," she replied wrapping her arms around my neck and her legs around my waist.

"What made you change your mind about us?" I inquired.

Her eyes looked over at my Annie who was staring at us and then she looked back to me and laughed.

"What the hell she do? Did she threaten you so that we could get back together?" I gritted.

"No! I told her what happened, and she gave me advice."

"Hell nah! What kind of advice did she give you? I already told you she crazy as hell. I don't need you acting like her," I let out nervously.

"I told her I wanted to put hands on your friend because she kept trying me. She told me that Kalyla is her niece but beat her ass if I have to." Zarie laughed.

"Yo, she told you that shit for real? You want to fight over a nigga?" I smiled.

"Nah, I want to fight her because she kept playing in my face, but we have an understanding so it shouldn't be a problem anymore," she murmured.

I needed to talk with my Annie because she bugged the fuck out if she thinks that pep talk she had with Zarie was about to fly.

There was a part of me that knew Kalyla wasn't really going to give up all the way on this little problem she has with Zarie, and I don't have time for my shorty throwing hands with my best friend.

"Yo, on some real shit, if you feel the need or want to fight Lyla, you would talk to me first, right?"

"No! You won't see it. She will get punched her in the mouth if she tries me again," she replied.

"Nah, that's not what's about to happen. I want you to keep an open mind about the situation. Don't go into a fresh start with fighting already on your mind. Do that for me please."

"Fine Kalen, just remember what I said."

"Man, you buggin'. Give me a kiss."

She playfully puckered up her lips, and I just shook my head laughing before placing my lips on hers.

****

One Week Later

I had just finished training and a nigga was tired as fuck. DiZarie said she had to study so I wasn't going to bother her for the time being. Shit, her studying was a good excuse for me to get some sleep. As soon as I stepped through the door, I kicked my shoes off, went straight to my room, and plopped down on the bed and my eyes started to slowly close.

Bzzz, Bzzz, Bzzz!

I felt around in my pocket for my phone, and when I fished it out, I glanced at the screen to see it was Zarie calling. I wasn't about to igg her call, so I answered and placed the phone of the side of my face closing eyes once again.

"What's up?" I answered.

"Are you busy? Can you help me study?" She asked.

"I don't know shit about no science, baby. I will be no help," I admitted.

"It's just reading me questions off of the cards and seeing if I know. I have it all made and ready to go. Pleaseeeeee, I cannot fail this class!" she begged.

"Aight, give me like an hour. I need to get some kind of sleep. I am exhausted as fuck."

"Oh, if you're too tired, don't worry about it. I'll get my mother or someone else to do it. I'll talk to you later," she replied before hanging up the phone.

Her ass didn't even give me a chance to tell her I just needed a couple of hours then I could help her. But shit, if she had someone else to do it I wasn't about to stop her right now. I will call her later though to see if she studied or if she still needed help with it.

Zobie

Working with Kalen's people was so much better than punching in at my old job. I haven't gone out on an assignment yet, and his grandfather was already blessing my account. This was the money I needed to help my moms out and get out here on my own. So, all this was perfect timing.

"Zobie, you like being around me, right? I'm not forcing you to do something you don't want to do, right?" Kalyla asked, sitting down on the couch next to me.

"Why wouldn't I want to be around you? We chillin'," I replied.

"I don't know. I guess because it seems like now, I'm all up in your personal space. Before it was Kalen and now that he has that little girlfriend, we don't hang out as much. So, I'm always talking to you or with you," she mentioned.

"True shit. I guess I need to start dodging your ass because you're only using a nigga. I am not going to be your Kalen replacement," I noted.

"What? That is not what I think of you Zobie, so don't do that. I've really enjoyed hanging out with you, and I wanted to ask you something."

"Yeah, and what's that?" I murmured, giving her my undivided attention.

"Would you date someone like me? Like I know I'm far from ugly, but I've noticed you never tried me."

"What? I never tried you? What the fuck does trying you consist of? A nigga has been into you, but I'm not on your radar. So maybe it's you," I countered.

"What does that mean? You would go out with me?"

"Kalyla, like you said you are a beautiful girl. Any nigga would be lucky to call you their girl. You need to be open to other niggas outside of the one you can't have," I informed.

"Who are you referring to? I don't have those kind of feelings for Kalen!" she snapped.

"Tell that to someone who doesn't know the two of you. But yeah, I would go out with you to answer your original question," I commented.

"So what's stopping you?" She questioned.

"The hell you talking about, Kalyla? Stop beating around the bush with what you want to ask me," I let out.

"I want to see what's up with us. I also don't want you to think I'm doing this because of how everything is. It's just a newfound thing with this. I see you in a different light. This isn't the same Zobie."

"Nah don't do that because I am the same person. You're just now paying attention to a nigga. Also, you don't want a relationship with me. We cool," I added.

She sucked her teeth and straddled my lap. The both of us were staring at one another and there was never a question about me feeling Lyla. She just wasn't about to play with me because she was trying to replace Kalen. Nah, that shit wasn't about to rock.

"Hell nah. Get yo ass up." I laughed.

She placed my face in her hands and kissed me. Aight, she's about to get her ass into something she ain't really ready for. My hands grabbed her soft ass as I opened my mouth accepting her tongue. My mind was telling me to put a stop to this shit, but the man in me was telling me to keep going until she stopped. Kalyla grinding her hips on top of me wasn't a good move.

"Yo, think about what you're doing," I warned, breaking the kiss.

"I want this," she replied placing her lips on mine again.

She didn't have to tell me twice. But when she went for my pants that was definitely not what I was expecting out of all of this. I was definitely about to bless her ass. I stood to my feet with her still in my arms. If she wanted the dick, then her ass was definitely going to get fucked. When we made it into her room, I laid her back onto the bed. I stared down at her as she rushed to take off her pants. She really wanted to get fucked. I was going to give it to her ass though.

"You sure?" I asked for clarification.

"Yes," she replied.

She didn't have to tell me the same thing twice. I took my pants and shoes off before walking over to the bed. I opened her legs and leaned down to kiss her.

"I'm a virgin so go slow." She informed me.

As soon as those words left her lips, my dick got soft. Hell nah, I wasn't about to do this shit with her ass. It was okay if this wasn't her first time. She was not thinking straight right now, and I wasn't about to be that nigga that took her virginity and wasn't sure where shit would go between us.

"Oh nah! We not about to do this," I declined as I put my pants back on.

"Wait. What? Why not? I want to do this," she disputed.

"Nah, because you not thinking right. I am not about to go there with you, and I know your ass is not really ready for that. It would be something different if this weren't your first time," I explained.

"Zobie! If I didn't want to do this, we wouldn't have made it this far!" She spat, sitting up on the bed.

"Nah, Lyla. Put your pants back on, and let's go watch a movie or some shit," I replied before walking out of her room.

Damn, why she had to be a virgin?

****

Kalen had hit a nigga up and told Kalyla and me to come to his spot because he ordered a couple of pizzas, and Zarie was over there. Kalyla still had an attitude, but her ass came along with us. We were now all sitting in the apartment quiet as fuck chomping down on our food. Kalen and his girl all up under each other on the couch while Kalyla sat mad far away from me with an attitude.

"What's wrong with y'all? The two of you quiet as fuck. Y'all good?" Kalen asked.

"Yeah, we good she's just—"

"No the hell we aren't. Who in their right mind wouldn't want to fuck me?" Kalyla spat.

Zarie spat out her drink and looked over at us with wide eyes. Kalen sat there with his mouth dropped open while I just shook my head in embarrassment.

"Damn, baby! Watch that shit," Kalen scolded.

"I am sooo sorry. I did not expect her to say that," Zarie apologized, blotting at the water on his shirt.

"True, try to keep that shit in your mouth next time," he said side eyeing her laughing.

"I will," she agreed, rolling her eyes and then kissed his lips.

I shook my head because this nigga Kalen was already acting like a little sap nigga around shorty.

"Now back to the two of y'all. What the fuck was that, Kalyla? I don't want to talk about you fuckin'! Wait, aren't you still a virgin?" Kalen laughed.

"It's not funny. Yes, I am, but that doesn't matter. I told him that I wanted to fuck! I mean I've done everything but stick his dick inside of me!" Kalyla spat.

"Yoo, you wild as fuck right now. Why you in here telling our damn business? That shit right there proves yo ass don't want or deserve no dick. The fuck wrong with you? We could have talked about that shit when we were alone," I grunted.

"No, it shouldn't be a conversation," Kalyla argued.

"I told you that I knew you weren't ready to go there. You will get that shit when I know you're ready!" I spat.

"Nigga, what kind of shit you on? How can you tell me I'm not ready? You don't know that shit, Zobie. As my nigga, you should want to fuck me. I mean what's stopping you from ripping my clothes off and fuckin' me like them niggas be doing to them hoes in the pornos?" She babbled.

"It's not about to happen until I say so. I mean I'm the nigga with the dick. Oh, and when the fuck did this shit become official? I'm not the nigga to play those type of games with. Ain't shit happening unless I know it's some real shit."

"How do you know my feelings aren't real? You're starting to piss me off right now," she gritted.

"Yall niggas are doing too much. Kalyla, ya ass not ready to be fuckin' nobody. You went all this long without fuckin', so you can wait a little while longer. Shit, wait until the nigga agree that the two of you are in a relationship," Kalen stated.

"Why are you telling her what to do with her body? I don't even see how the two of you can tell her what she's ready for when she was willingly giving you her body. If it was the other way around, you would low key be mad," Zarie noted.

"Hell nah! I know her ass is trying to use me. Everything has shifted with you being added to the group. Now that she doesn't have Kalen to sit around and be up under, we spend a lot of time together. She is finally noticing a nigga and wants me, but she is rushing shit. I fuck with her the hard way and fuck yeah, I'll fuck her in all kinds of ways, but she's not ready for all that. Right now, we can chill, and when I feel like she's ready for that, she will get the dick," I uttered.

"Okay, soo can we move on from the two of you fuckin' I don't want to hear about it anymore."

"Are y'all fuckin?" Kalyla questioned, pointing between Zarie and Kalen.

"Why is that any of your business?" Zarie sassed.

"Oh thought we were all having an open discussion about sex. Excuse me," Kalyla murmured, throwing her hands up.

"You are so damn mean yo. You did not have to snap like that," Kalen scolded, pulling at Zarie's hair.

"Nigga, I told you to stop pulling my hair. I wasn't trying to be mean, but damn. I didn't ask about their sex life. It was volunteered," Zarie argued.

"Man, y'all doing the most. I'm about to head to my crib. I'm tired as fuck. I got no sleep after training," I announced standing to my feet.

"What do y'all do? What are y'all in training for?" Zarie inquired.

"Ahh, that's something you don't need to know. Everything is all good," Kalen replied.

He was not telling her and I didn't have anything to say. I cleaned up my mess and went to the door to wait for Kalyla to get her shit together. Once she came to the door, I threw up my hands with a head nod, and we were out the door.

"Aye, I'll see you later," I informed her as she arrived at the front of her door.

"Fine," she said with an attitude.

"You will live to see another day." I laughed before kissing her forehead and stood there waiting for her to get inside her apartment.

Once she was inside, and I heard the locks click I turned to leave so that a nigga could go home.

DiZarie

"**B**aby I'm tired as fuck. How many more questions you have to go over?" Kalen complained.

After Zobie and Kalyla left, we cleaned up his place and went to his room so that he could help me study. Honestly, this was the only reason I came over here because he told he would help me study. Now here we are both laying in his bed and his ass is complaining about reading the questions to me.

"Come on, Kalen! We have to get through this stack. You told me that you were going to help me out. Let's get through this stack, please," I pleaded.

"Aight sooo the first question is… What is wobble hypothesis? What is the importance of wobble and degeneracy? What the fuck kind of shit is wobble hypothesis? Is this the right set of cards?" He asked, flipping the card over.

"Yes, it's the right cards! Why is that in there? That was all the way in the beginning of the semester. Damn umm, wobble hypothesis. Umm we gotta come back to that one." I laughed.

"Man, you don't know these damn questions. Aight, let me put this on the side. Next question, which amino acid is the primary source of ammonia?" He read out loud.

"Tyrosine," I answered.

"Ayee!! You know something, I see," he praised as he looked at the back of the card.

"Don't try to play me. Go on to the next question," I instructed, laughing.

"If a chemical reaction has a positive change in enthalpy and a positive change in the entropy, then what will happen?"

"What the fuck? Umm, it will never be spontaneous."

"Umm..."

"Wait, no!!! It will be spontaneous at high temperatures," I corrected.

"Okay, I see you. Let's do another question," he announced, flipping through the cards.

I moved closer to him and laid my head on his shoulder and had half of my body on his. Getting comfortable in his arms, he flipped through the cards with me occasionally telling him to go to the next card since I already knew the answers.

"Bae, you know almost all this shit what are you trying to study?" He asked still flipping.

"I just need to make sure I know all of this before my exam in the morning," I yawned.

"Aight so another question. Um, you know this one already?" he asked, showing me the question.

"Yeah, go to the next one," I yawned.

"Yo ass better not go to sleep. All that damn yawning you doing right now." He laughed.

"I am so tired, but I need to get home, and I need to finish studying," I replied.

"Aight bet. Let's get through these questions though."

I snuggled closer to him sleepy and answering of the questions he called out.

****

Ring, Ring, Ring!

I jumped up out of my sleep searching around for my phone to shut the alarm off. Once the alarm was off, and I had come to, it made me realized where the hell I was. I gasped and jumped up off the bed looking back at a sleeping Kalen. What the hell? I don't have time to get home and get to class on time for this exam. How could I sleep here? What the fuck?

"Ughh!! Kalen, get up!" I panicked, shaking him awake.

He sat up with his eyes halfway open and confusion all over his face.

"Can I borrow some of your clothes?" I asked.

"What?" He replied still tired as hell.

I shook my head and just decided to help myself to his clothes. I grabbed a pair of his sweat pants and a t-shirt before rummaging through his draws to get some socks. When I opened the draw, and I said a silent thank you lord when I saw an in open pack of underwear too. Kalen was on the skinnier side, so I hope like hell these little extra hips I had could fit these underwear.

I grabbed up everything and rushed off to his bathroom. I didn't know where shit was located, but that wasn't going to stop me from looking. Opening and shutting different doors and cabinet drawers, I find everything I needed, even an extra toothbrush.

I quickly hopped in the shower doing my daily morning routine but in less time. I had to get all the way to the other side of town just to get to school. After a good shower and making sure everything else was straight, I threw on the clothes along with my socks. My hair was all over the place right now, but I know I had to have a comb and brush inside of my car. So that could get handled while I was in class. I ran out to his bathroom, put my sneakers on, and I was ready. I grabbed my phone and went to the other side of the bed kissing Kalen's lips a couple of time before rushing out of his apartment trying to make it to class.

****

"Whew!" I exclaimed, walking out of Professor Dear's classroom.

That damn test was hard as fuck, but I was confident that I did excellent on that test. Oh, and truth be told that damn test had the wobble hypothesis one there. Thank the lord, I read over that chapter again before going into class.

"Aye, DiZarie wait up!" I heard from behind me.

I turned around to see Keith rushing towards me. I stopped in my tracks and waited for Keith to catch up with me. Keith was cool as fuck. He was fine as hell too and asked me out a few times. Even though he was fine as fuck, he gave me fairy tendencies. I asked him one time too, and he denied it, so all I could do was take his word. Anyway, when he made it in front of me, I sized him up and took him in. Keith had dark cocoa skin that was far from blemish free. Even with the acne, he still looked good as hell.

He had them lips niggas called soup coolers. There were black as hell though, which told me he smoked. He stood to be around five nine or five ten. He wasn't very tall. Keith was also on the husky side. He wasn't fat, but he definitely a buff ass nigga. I could tell that he worked out. The way he dressed wasn't impressive, but I will admit that I didn't try that hard when it came to dress either.

"Aye, so you want to go get some lunch or something? I'm done with all my classes today, so I have nothing else to do." He asked.

"I'm sorry maybe another time. My mother has been blowing up my phone because I haven't been home. I ended up falling asleep at my boyfriend house last night, and she has been worried sick. I need to go and see her so she can see that I am alive and okay. After that, I need to go get my school stuff from his house," I informed.

"Wait you have a boyfriend? Was it that nigga that came up to the school causing a scene?" He inquired.

"Yeah, that's Kalen." I smiled.

"Oh damn, I thought that didn't work out. Weren't you telling me about this issue you had with his people?"

"Yeah, well not everybody. It was just his best friend and her mother that had a problem with me. Everything all good right now," I assured.

"Oh damn. Aight well if you change your mind about doing something, just hit me up. I'll see you around, pretty Zee," he crooned before strolling off.

I stood there confused for a second before shrugging my shoulders and walking over to my car. As soon as my butt hit the seat,

I threw my bookbag in the back and pulled out my phone to go over the messages that I didn't respond to.

Ma: *DiZarie! Where the hell are you? Your daddy and I are worried sick. Please call me, so I know that you are okay*

Ma: *Zarie, I don't like this. Please answer your phone.*

Ma: *DIZARIE BELLMON!! I am going to fuck you up!*

Ma: *You better not be ignoring me so that you can have sex with your little boyfriend.*

Daddy: *DiZarie!! If you are with that little nigga you call a boyfriend, we are going to have a problem. Hit me back ASAP.*

Kalen: *Yo you couldn't wake a nigga up to tell me that you were leaving? Hit me up and let me know what you plan on doing later. Good luck on your test, nerd.*

I smiled at his message and then went back to my mother name so that I can call her.

"DIZARIE!!!!! What the hell took you so long to contact us? I cannot believe you. DiZarie, this is really irresponsible." My mother scolded as soon as she answered the phone.

"Ma, I'm sorry. Kalen was helping me study last night, and I ended up falling asleep at his place. When my alarm went off in the morning, I saw I had overslept. I didn't have time to do nothing but get ready and rush to school. I had my exam with Professor Dear today, and we all know she doesn't play about being late to class," I explained.

"Are you having sex?" she asked.

"What!! Ma, please don't do that. I really just fell asleep. Nothing but studying happened," I assured.

"Well, still you and that boy getting cozy with each other. I know I can't stop you from having sex with him so just make sure you're using protection," she replied.

"Ma! I am not about to talk about this with you. Besides I'm twenty-one and I'm pretty sure I already know about having safe sex. I'm on my way home, so I'll see you in a bit."

"Yeah and when you get home, we will have a talk about all of this," she noted.

"Ma, I am not about to talk about this. If I decided to have sex, I would make sure I'm safe and can we just leave it at that," I pleaded.

"Aight, well I'm relieved to hear you are okay. All I ask is that you keep me up to date with everything if you decide to stay out again."

"Ugh, alright, ma," I groaned.

"Alright later, love you. I'll tell your daddy that I spoke with you," she replied before disconnecting the call.

I shook my head and threw my phone to the side and pulled out of my school parking lot. I was about to go back home and get in the bed so I can get some more sleep.

Ring, Ring, Ring!

I pressed the button on my steering wheel to answer the phone call.

"Hello?" I answered.

"I know you saw my text!" Kalen spat.

"You have a problem. I did see your text, and I didn't think it needed a response." I laughed.

"Why you like playing with a nigga? Where you at? What are you about to do?" he quizzed.

"I'm about to take me a bomb ass nap. I am out of school for the summer, and I can finally relax," I gushed.

"Why you don't come over here? I'm done training for the day," he suggested.

"Kalen, are you going to let me sleep? I am sooo tired, oh and you can't let me sleep all day. My mother and father went crazy last night when I didn't go home."

"Oh shit, what they say?" he asked.

"My moms tried to talk to me about sex. They were doing the most all because I fell asleep while studying."

"Ahhhh!" He screamed into the phone laughing.

He would think that shit was funny.

"Aye, come on so that we can take a nap together," he murmured.

Oh, he didn't have to tell me twice. His deep voice had a bitch already redirecting my route to his place. Since everything was back on between us, it's been a different vibe. It wasn't him trying all the time with me. I wasn't against this relationship. The few days we spent apart after he called, it was weird. I didn't even know how much I enjoyed talking to him until it all stopped. Then talking with my mother and his aunt about the reason why we stopped gave me some clarity. Even though I still have my eyes on ole girl, she wasn't going to get any more energy from me. All I was going to worry about is what's going on between Kalen and I. Shorty and anyone else doesn't matter to me.

****

"It took yo ass long enough to get here," Kalen greeted.

I stood outside of his door with my arms folded and my face all frowned up. Kalen laughed and pulled me into his apartment wrapping his arm around my neck and playfully kissing the side of my face.

"Ma, you always frowning. Why you got my shit on, shorty?" He laughed.

"Because I had nothing else to wear. I should have worn some shorts because it is hot as fuck out there." I groaned.

He shook his head closing and locking the door as I made my way towards his room. I decided I needed to text my moms and let her know I decided to come here instead of going home so that ,she won't panic like they did last night.

Me: *Ma I am with Kalen. I definitely will be home tonight.*

Ma: *DiZarie, are y'all having sex? Are you taking your birth control?*

Me: *Maaaaaaaaaaaa! Please stop.*

I wasn't about to tell her I stopped taking birth control after reading up on the one that I was taking. To be honest, I wasn't taking any kind of birth control anymore. For one I wasn't having sex, and for two whenever we get to that point, all I can do is hope I don't get caught up.

"I thought you were so tired?" Kalen said, walking into his room.

He climbed into his bed, and I followed right behind him. I was not going to be up for long. He settled in the bed, and instantly I snuggled closer to him, and my eyes started to drift.

"Aye, so how did that test go?" He asked, causing my eyes to pop back open.

"Um, it went good. That damn wobble hypothesis was on there too. Good thing I read over that chapter right before the test. I knew everything else for the most part," I said, yawning.

"I know you not that tired. Sit up with me for a little bit," he demanded.

"Nooo! Kalen, you said you would let me sleep. I am tired sir. We can talk when I wake back up." I groaned.

"Zarie," he called out.

I looked up at him with my eyes half open. He laughed and shook his head before kissing my lips and telling me I could go to sleep. Shoot, he didn't have to say it again because I was going to sleep anyway.

****

"KALEN!" I heard someone shout and my eyes shot up.

The both of us woke up out of our sleep looking around the room confused as hell. I instantly got pissed when I saw Kalyla's ass walking into his room. What the fuck is she doing here?

"Oh, my bad. I didn't know she was still here," she exclaimed.

"Damn Lyla, why you didn't just call?" He groaned laying back down, pulling me closer to him.

While this nigga was trying to go to sleep, I sat up staring at ole girl with the stale face. With it clear as day that we are trying to sleep, her ass still stood in the doorway staring.

"Come on. Let's go back to sleep," he groaned, pulling on my body again.

"Kalen, get up!" I snapped, nudging him.

"Gah damn what? A nigga is tired as fuck. Kalyla, I will talk to your ass later man. Go!" He snapped.

She looked at me with a smirk on her face and rolled her eyes before leaving out of his room. Here that bitch was talking about making peace, but here she goes with this shit. I am sick of this shit. This is exactly why I said, that I wasn't about to be friends with this girl. Yesterday she was begging for dick from Zobie and now here she is all over here in my nigga's face. Kalen and I definitely need to discuss this apartment access shit.

Kalyla

I know I said I would try with that girl, but damn I can't help myself. I really don't get what Kalen sees in her ass. This bitch is sleeping over now, and he had the nerve to put me out his place. Kalen was definitely acting brand new because of this hoe. I hit my mother up to talk with her about this, and she told me she was at home with my aunts chilling. I didn't want to talk about this in front of them, but if anyone knew about Kalen, it would be auntie Ny. I was pulling up to the house, and all my aunts were here, even Kalen's mom Lou was here. This was about to be so embarrassing, but I needed advice.

I got out of my car and went into the house. I could hear all of them in the kitchen laughing and most likely gossiping about who knows what.

"That girl's got Kalen wide open. I like her though. She has a little attitude to her," I heard Auntie Ny admit.

"But everyone knows he is just playing with that girl's feelings. He knows he wants to be with Kalyla," my mother argued.

"He has been adamant about not wanting to go there with Kalyla. Get over it. That nigga knows what the fuck he wants and it's not her," Auntie Ny retorted.

"Dang, you ain't have to say it like that," I sneered, entering the kitchen.

Everyone turned towards the doorway as I entered the kitchen.

"Oh hey, baby! I didn't know you were coming." My mother greeted.

"Well, I wanted your advice with this situation, but I see y'all already talking shit about me," I ranted.

"Well shit, it's the truth. Are you coming here to admit that you're in love with Kalen, or are you still frontin'?" Auntie Ny challenged.

"I don't know how I feel. All I know is that girl came into the picture and Kalen is acting different. I don't like that hoe, and she needs to leave him alone. I don't even see what he sees in her. Kalen's acting brand new," I grunted.

"This is a new side of Kalen you are seeing. You so used to him curving girls he really didn't want and now that he has actual feelings for someone, you don't like it. You need to find you someone or distance yourself. I told that girl if I were her I would have been dragged you," Auntie Ny admitted.

"You told her what?" I fumed.

"Listen, you're my niece and all, but baby, what you're doing to that girl isn't right. They both like each other, and I noticed the change when Kalen first talked to us about her. This was definitely someone he is into. Don't say you want him because he's happy with someone else. I see you been hanging out with Zobie. Why don't you date him? He's a handsome little something," Auntie Ny noted.

"Zobie, doesn't want to be with me," I disputed.

"How do you know? I've seen the way he looks at you," Auntie Jana added.

"She's so stuck on a dick that she can't have," Auntie Ny muttered.

"Why the fuck she can't have him, Nyrae? I'm tired of y'all trying to play my daughter. We all know he wants to be with her. I don't know why y'all sitting here trying to convince us that he doesn't

when you don't even believe that shit!" My mother bellowed.

"I know that they have been around each other since they were

six years old and not once did he try something with her. Damn, I

know that should tell you all something. Camille, I've been meaning

to say something to you about how you treated that girl too. This shit

is something between them, not your old ass. Mind your business.

Kalyla, you better stop before you push him all the way out of your

life. He likes that girl! He is in a relationship with that girl. Girl, if

they end up having sex, that's it for you. That nigga is really going to

be all up on her," Auntie Ny sassed.

"I didn't come over here for all that. I thought y'all would help

me get her out the picture!" I barked.

"Why would I do that? Did you not hear me tell you I told that

girl to beat ya ass the next time you tried her? Girl, I love you but you

are doing the most. If you weren't doing the most, you could hang out

with him more. You need to learn about the power of pussy. If you

continue with this shit, and they start fuckin', you can forget about chillin' with him again. I suggest you chill out and fuck with Zobie," Auntie Ny continued.

"Nyrae, I'm not about to let you keep disrespecting my daughter. Kalyla, do you want to be with Kalen or are you just doing this because you want to continue to have him all to yourself?" My mother asked.

"I don't know," I admitted.

"Well, leave their relationship alone. Even though I feel like you really know, I'm not going to keep asking you. Let that boy live," my mother scolded.

I came over here for no reason. I don't give a damn what they say. Kalen needs to learn how to better handle having a stupid ass girlfriend and me in his life. I shouldn't have been the one pushed off to the side.

****

"Yo!" Kalen answered.

"Nigga, don't answer your phone like that. What are you doing? You want to watch some movies? I'm bored, and Zobie isn't answering his phone," I replied.

"I was just about to text you. We were about to chill at the crib and play some games. Zobie is here already with Zarie and me. Come down the hall," he invited.

"I don't think I want to come down there. I'll probably just go to sleep," I declined.

"Man, what's wrong with you? Come on. Stop playing."

"I'm not playing. I'm just going to chill at my spot. Umm, I guess I'll talk to you later," I huffed and hung up the phone.

I was not about to have a game night with them niggas. The nerve of his ass to try and invite me to that shit anyway. After that so-called talk that I had with my moms and aunts, I was in my feelings. I can admit that shit. Like all of them were supposed to be on my side. Shit, I should have known that it was going go that way with Nyrae because she will forever be team Kalen, but everyone else could have been on my side. That shit was fucked up.

"Kalyla!!" Kalen yelled when he entered my apartment.

I had nothing to say to his ass, so I just threw my comforter over my head.

"Yo faking ass not sleep. What the hell wrong with you?" Kalen yelled, jumping on my bed.

"Ugh!! Get the fuck off me, Kalen. Why are you here? I thought you were having a fun time with your girlfriend," I cringed.

"I thought we were all good. What the hell is wrong with you?" he questioned, ripping the covers back.

"Nothing I just don't feel like being around a whole bunch of people. Since you started dating shorty, we don't do anything together. I wanted to chill, laugh, and watch movies like we use to," I complained.

"You don't like Zarie, why? If you try to get to know her, everything will be all good."

"Kalen, I don't want to get to know that girl. Fuck her. Like on some real shit. You didn't see how she was acting towards me earlier when I stopped by your place. She said she wouldn't be rude or whatever, and that girl is still holding a grudge. So, I'm just going to chill out on all things you while you're still with her," I vowed.

"You buggin' come down there and play some games. Zarie is not worried about you. Stop being so damn evil and come on," he urged.

"Nah I'm just going to chill here. You say one thing, but the way she was looking at me earlier told me something else," I disputed.

"This shit is getting real corny. How the fuck are you supposed to be my best friend, and you can't be happy for a nigga. That shit is real fucked up. She isn't the one that's causing us not to chill together, it's you, and for the life of me, I can't understand why. Maybe what everyone has been saying is true. If that is, I don't really know what to tell you. I am not trying to go that route with you. If that's a problem and you can accept that then maybe we need to keep this space between us," he proposed.

"Wooow! Here this girl comes and you all of a sudden think I'm in love with you. Nigga, please get over yourself," I snorted.

"Well shit, prove me wrong. You are acting real different right now. You are going to another level with your shit now. I'm confused as fuck right now. I don't know what's going on with you right now, but it's whatever, I guess. I'm about to get out of here. I guess I'll see you around," he muttered, getting off my bed.

Man fuck Kalen. I can't believe his ass just basically tried to play me.

"Can you tell Zobie that I need him," I sneered.

"Yeah, whatever!" he snapped, walking out of my room.

I can't believe we are at this point in our friendship.

Kalen

The nerve of Kalyla, this shit she was doing was getting old as fuck. When DiZarie told me how Kalyla looked at her earlier, I told her that she was being paranoid or just picking because Kalyla was the one that extended the truce this time around. However, the talk I just had with her ass wasn't the same person who was just trying to be friends with Zarie at the damn cookout. The shit was tiring trying to get her ass to at least give DiZarie a damn try without judging her. With the way she was acting, I had to start assessing everything. I kept trying to dispute the notion that Kalyla was feeling a nigga, but shit, that seems to be the only answer on why she was acting like this. Hopefully, us spending some time apart will give her ass some clarity that our relationship was strictly a brother and sister type of shit.

"Where's Kalyla? Is she bringing her stubborn ass down here?" Zobie asked as soon as I re-entered my apartment.

"Hell nah, her ass is not coming. She also told me to tell you she needed you," I gritted.

"What the hell happened down there?" He quizzed.

"Man, she's your problem now. She really does want you to go to her place," I informed.

"Wait, what do you mean she's my problem? Nigga, that's your best friend," he shot back.

"Nah, I don't know who that is. I'm tired of trying to convince her ass of something simple. She was the one that extended the truce with my girl, but she still has a problem. I don't know what the hell she wants me to do," I declared, throwing my hands up.

"Y'all are doing the most. Aye, I'm going to go and see what's up with this damn girl. Aight Zarie, see you around shorty. Kalen, you know you aren't letting this shit go. You and Kalyla need to get y'all shit together," Zobie grumbled before leaving my place.

I plopped down on the couch while Zarie stood on the other side of the living with a scowl on her face. I didn't need her damn attitude right now because I already had to go through that shit with Kalyla for no gah damn reason. Who the fuck knew that me wanting to be in a serious ass relationship would cause these many problems?

"So, what you want to do? We can still play some of these games, or we can kick our feet up and watch some movies," I said, wiping my hand down my face.

"Um, we can watch a movie, I guess. Are you okay?" Zarie probed.

"Yup," I replied.

Picking up the remote, I turned on the TV and flipped through the firestick to find something for us to watch.

"Are you sure?" She questioned.

"Yeah! Why the fuck you asking me again like I lied or some shit?" I snapped.

"See! This isn't what you're about to do. I didn't do shit to you nigga. Whatever problems you have with ole girl, take that shit up with her!" She spat back.

"Why the fuck are you trying to argue with a nigga? All we need to do is sit the fuck down and watch a movie," I gritted.

"Whatever, nigga. I'm going home. You're not about to take your anger out on me when I haven't done shit to you. Everything was all good before you went to go talk to her!" She roared.

I don't have time to go back and forth with her ass. She stormed off to the back, and I sat in the same spot going through the different movies. If her ass wanted to leave, then fine. I wasn't about to chase behind her ass. Between her and Kalyla, they both had me fucked up. Minutes later DiZarie came from the back with her things in her arms, and she stormed past me all the way to my apartment door.

"DiZarie, don't you leave your ass out this apartment," I gritted.

I wasn't going to get up and go after her physically, but she knew what's up.

"Nah, fuck that Kalen because you're definitely trying me, nigga. I don't give a fuck what happened between you two. I'm not her, so fix your fuckin' attitude, nigga!" She snapped, yanking the door up and running right into my grandfather and falling to the floor.

"Ahh fuck!" she shouted as she got up.

All I could do was laugh because she still hasn't looked up to see who she ran into. She was too busy picking her stuff up and cursing like there was no tomorrow.

"I'm sorry about that, baby girl," P. Storm apologized, handing Zarie the rest of her papers.

When she heard his voice, she finally looked up, and her hand went over her mouth.

"I am so sorry. I normally don't speak like this in front of older people. My mother and father taught me better than that. I was not watching where I was going. I really do apologize," Zarie ranted.

"Yo, that's what you get for being dramatic and trying to leave. Bring yo ass back in here." I laughed.

"I don't see anything funny, Kalen. I'm going home. You want to have an attitude, well you can do that here alone."

"Man, come on and sit down," I coaxed.

"Nah! You can sit in here with the sour face by yourself!" she snapped, trying to leave out.

P. Storm put his arm up stopping her from leaving.

"I need to talk to the both of you," he asserted.

"Talk to me for what?" Zarie asked.

"Sit down, and you will find out," P. Storm said, closing the door.

Hesitantly Zarie sat down on the couch and tried to create space between us. I shook my head and pulled her closer to me. P. Storm grabbed a chair and sat in front of us just staring. I had no clue what he wanted to talk to us about, but it had to be something series if he just popped up here without calling first.

"What's going on?" I inquired.

"Do you know who her family is?" He questioned, pointing towards Zarie.

"Yeah! I met them before too," I admitted.

"Does your family know who his family is?" He questioned Zarie.

"Um, I'm not sure. I know my father and uncle talked to him before. Why is there a problem?" Zarie retorted.

"What does your family do to make their money?" P. Storm challenged.

"My father owns a construction company and real estate company. My mother owns a chain of hair salons here and down south. Why?" Zarie asked.

"That's all you know?" P. Storm wondered.

"If you have a direct question, ask it. I don't know what you're getting at right now," Zarie hissed.

"What's with all the questions, P. Storm?" I cut in.

"The questions are because the two families are currently at war over territory," P. Storm gritted, staring Zarie down.

"Excuse me? Are you sure? My people would have said something by now. I know my daddy already looked into Kalen by now. He hasn't said anything," Zarie objected.

"Are you sure about that? Young lady, I don't play when it comes to my children and grandchildren. You are a beautiful girl, but if I find out you on some other shit, I will kill your whole family," P. Storm threatened.

"Whoa! P. Storm, what was that? I think you're getting shit mixed up. I've met her people, and there wasn't an issue. Y'all really trippin' out on me being with someone," I interrupted.

"Nah, you heard what I said. Maybe the two of you need to call off whatever this is. I don't trust her," he declared.

"What is with your family disrespecting me? Listen, sir, I don't strive to disrespect my elders, but come on now. I don't get why y'all keep trying to play me. My family is definitely not worried about him at all. Also, I don't need him for anything. I don't get where this whole trust thing is coming from when you don't even know me," Zarie defended.

"Aight, I heard all that, but at the end of the day, this might now be a good fit. You're into books and shit while he's going a different path in life," P. Storm replied.

"Come on. Tell me what the real problem is! What different path he's taking?" Zarie spat.

"He's in training to do assignments, more specifically hire to kill."

"Oh, so you're telling me I need to start carrying while I'm around him? I'm lost on why you're saying all of this," Zarie gritted.

"You know how to shoot a gun?" I quizzed.

"I'm trained just in case," she replied.

"Wait. What? Just in case what?" I probed.

Oh, I needed to know this because this never came up before. Shit, I didn't know she knew about guns.

"I don't know. If something happens, I guess. My uncle Juju use to be in the streets. So, Riah and I are trained to use a gun. I also have a blade on me at all times," she admitted.

"What the fuck? No, you don't," I denied.

"I don't what?" she asked.

"Keep a blade on you at all times."

She bent down, and when she came back up, sure enough, her ass had a big ass blade in her hand. She flicked her wrist doing some trick before that shit was gone.

"The fuck kind of Houdini shit you on. Where you put that shit?" I asked, looking around.

"Wouldn't you like to know. Now, I'm not sure what was told to you about me, but I wouldn't do anything to hurt him." DiZarie assured.

"Nah, I was lying about all that. My daughter came and talked to me about you. She told me she liked you and you had heart. That says a lot coming from Nyrae. I had to check you out for myself. I do have a proposition for you," P. Storm announced.

"Yo, why you playing games. Y'all don't want a nigga to be in a relationship," I shot.

"Ah shut yo ass up. She ain't going nowhere. I know you're in school and all, but how would you like to train?" P. Storm proposed.

"Excuse me? What am I training for?" Zarie asked.

"That shit you just did with that blade piqued my interest. You would be perfect as an in case of emergency stand-in."

"Oh no! That's not what I'm trying to do," Zarie declined.

"It's not like you don't know how to shoot a gun already unless you were lying before." He shot back.

"Oh no, I wasn't lying, but that's not what I'm about to do," DiZarie asserted.

"What's the problem with going to training?" P. Storm wondered.

"It's not my field of work, so why should I train. I know what I need to know."

"There isn't anything wrong with learning more. Come with him for the rest of this week, and if you don't want to do it anymore, I'll leave it alone. I will even pay you like I do them for your time," P. Storm proposed, leaning forward and extending his hand.

DiZarie started at him for a second and looked back at me. She cut her eyes back to P. Storm before reluctantly shaking his hand in agreement.

"I'll see you tomorrow, Ms. DiZarie. Kalen, walk with me downstairs," P. Storm announced standing to his feet.

"Aye, find a movie. I'll be right back," I said as I followed my grandfather out of my apartment.

"Little nigga," P. Storm groaned.

"What was that in there? Do you not really trust her?" I quizzed.

"Honestly I was trying to test her. I like her. You may have a problem on your hands with that one," he informed.

"Wait, why you say that?" I asked.

"You don't have to go all the way downstairs with me, but she reminds me of your aunt. That's why Nyrae like her ass so much. She's a bit quieter than Nyrae, but the look in her eyes. Ohh, I know it oh so well." He laughed.

"Wait, what you mean by that? Do you think she's crazy like my Annie? Do I need to sleep with one eye open?" I interrogated.

"Calm down lil nigga. Just don't fuck her over. She's a real one. Why do you think I invited her to train? I see it all in her."

"P. Storm you can't say all this and try to leave," I disputed.

"Relax chill with your girl. She's a good one to have on your team so do right by her," he said, getting onto the elevator.

"Aight."

"See y'all in the morning!" He said before the elevator doors closed.

Damn, he came over here and shook everything up. It turns out that I don't know shit about DiZarie really. Why the fuck didn't I know her uncle used to be in the streets?

Zobie

"**N**ow he's bringing her to training with him. This is ridiculous. Does this bitch has to be everywhere," Kalyla complained.

"Man, that girl ain't worried about you. Go on and let's do the training. Stop worrying about her!" I growled.

Since Kalen walked in with DiZarie this morning, her ass has been complaining. We haven't gotten through not one simulation because she was so damn pressed with what DiZarie was doing. This shit was getting ridiculous.

"Aye Zobie, switch with Kalen for me. Do the last simulation with DiZarie. I want to see something," Storm ordered.

"Um, okay cool," I replied, walking over to where Kalen and DiZarie were standing.

"Heyy Zobie. I saw you were busy, so I didn't want to bother you," DiZarie greeted.

"Yeah, I didn't get much done since I got here, but Storm wants me and you to do the last simulation together. Shit, it would be the only one I got done today," I griped.

"Oh um, okay. Lead the way."

"Wait, why is he having y'all do this together? Who am I going to be paired with? I have to do target practice or something?" Kalen asked.

"Nah, you and Kalyla will get the first simulation done. She hasn't gotten shit done today, and she's not leaving until she gets it done. Go ahead and suit up with her," Storm ordered.

"Oh no, I don't feel like being around her right now. I can go through on my own," Kalen dismissed.

"I wasn't asking you. The two of you are family, so get over it and go over there to get to work," Storm demanded and walked off.

"See, I should have known this shit was going to happen," Kalen grumbled, walking over to Kalyla.

"Well, the simulation is over this way. You know how to shoot a gun shorty?" I joked.

"Yeah. Why do you think I'm here? I am too nice with a gun," she boasted.

"Whatever let go. There are twelve targets in here and three innocent bystanders. Put these on and let's get ready," I instructed.

She nodded her head in agreement and placed the cans on her ears. I looked back at her, and she nodded her head telling me she was ready. I kicked in the door, and it was time for action. The first cut out popped out, and before I could even get a shot out, the target was hit. Damn, I wanted to look back, but we still had to go through. On the way to another room, another person popped out. I lowered my weapon when I saw that it was a bystander. Continuing with the stimulation, I was really surprised. DiZarie was actually good as fuck with a gun. With how she was going on, I was only able to get five kills out of the assignment. That was not what I expected.

"Damn, so you nice for real," I complimented.

"I should be with how much my uncle had me in a gun range. Doing stuff like this is fun though." She gleamed.

"You think this shit is fun? This is some real concentration. One wrong move can make a whole operation go wrong," I voiced.

"I know that but you also never know what can happen. So, either way, I enjoyed this. Shooting long range is so much better." She shrugged

She walked over to the table where the guns were laid out and skillfully took apart her Ruger SR9.

"Is this about to be a permanent thing or is it just for today?" I probed.

"I honestly don't know. I believe I'm just doing this because his grandfather asked me."

"So, are you thinking about doing assignments?"

"What? No, I'm going to continue on my original career path. I'm doing this for whatever reason his grandfather asked me to do it for. I really don't fully understand why he asked me to show up," she admitted.

"Oh okay. Did you want to do another simulation? There is one for long range shooting," I suggested.

"Oh yeah, that's cool with me." Zarie shrugged.

I glad Storm did this switch because I was about to knock out all these simulations.

****

"So, I saw you enjoying your time with little miss perfect DiZarie," Kalyla childishly murmured.

"I went through with my training. We could have gotten something done together if you weren't so pressed over shorty. You really need to grow up," I scolded.

"Yeah, whatever. Today was my last day going to those stupid ass training classes," she announced.

"Your grandfather is giving you the money to open your business now?" I quizzed.

"Last time I check Storm wasn't my grandfather," she sneered.

"What? You are talking stupid right now. After all these years, Storm isn't your grandfather now. You bugged the fuck out," I hissed.

"I ain't doing shit but speaking facts. I'm thinking about going to the south and be with my real family."

"What? You're really doing all of this because of his girlfriend? You are so damn dramatic."

"Yeah, if you say so. I would love for you just to drop me off and just go about your business," she sniped.

She didn't have to tell me twice. She wanted to act like a spoiled brat, so I'll let her have her little tantrum. When I pulled up in front of their building, her childish ass tried to get out of the car while the car was still moving. As soon as she slammed my door, I pulled off on her ass. The way she acts is because everyone around her babies her ass. She had the nerve to say she wanted more with me. The fuck I look like getting myself into some shit like that. Kalyla needed to grow the fuck up.

DiZarie

One Month Later

Strangely enough things between Kalen and I have been going great. The only thing I've noticed is that he's always checking his phone. I honestly think he's waiting for Kalyla to say she been trippin' so that they can start hanging out again, but shorty wasn't giving in. I tried to convince him to go and talk to her, but he wasn't trying to give in either. Both of them were being dramatic as fuck if you asked me. This was what I didn't want to happen. I was coming in between their relationship, and I didn't feel good about it. Oh and by him not hanging out with her, we spend just a little bit too much time together.

Shoot, I had to lie to him today just so that I could get some alone time. I told him my mother wanted me to spend some time with her. Even though that was true, that was something I had no plans on doing. I see her ass at night, so we didn't need to hang out right now. I took this day today to have me some good ole me time. Today I went to the mall to buy a few things. Sad to say but the way I dressed did change a bit. My mother and Kalen had pointed it out last week, and it really bothered me. My mother says it's because I'm in a relationship, but my aunt told me it's just me growing out of my baggy phase. I loved my aunt's reasoning better.

Anyway, today was about me relaxing and getting centered with myself again. I went to the gym this morning well, only after I had to basically convince Kalen and his grandfather I wasn't going to this dumb training. After yoga, I was able to take a relaxing bath. I was able to meditate. Kalen wasn't blowing up my phone since he thought I was chilling with my mother. It was just a peaceful day overall. I was done shopping, and now I was sitting in Red Robin about to have a nice dinner with myself. I was in the mood for a good ass burger.

"Hi, my name is Tyeisha, and I will be your server today. Did you have a chance to look over the menu and choose what you would like today?"

"Hi, um not fully, but I know what I want, so can I just like build my own burger?" I questioned.

"Sure. What would you like?"

"Okay so I like the size of this monster burger, but I want the fried onions sautéed mushrooms and peppers. Green peppers to be exact. I want some bacon of course. I also want something with avocado on it so maybe just choose a separate burger that has that on there. Umm, oh and I want the lettuce, tomatoes, pickles, and all that on there. I know I'm not going to eat all this, but those chili cheese fries look good in the picture. Have you ever had them?"

"Um, I don't think I've had that before. However, I will admit that it's a best seller. You can do like a half size just in case you don't like it," she suggested.

"Okay cool. That would be good. I probably shouldn't mix alcohol with any of this but…"

"Nope, too much grease," she cut in laughing.

"Okay. Give me one of these freckled lemonades," I finished, closing out my menu and handing the menu back to the server.

"Okay, I'll put your order in and come back with your drink and appetizer shortly."

"Thank you."

She left my table and went to check over my notifications. I saw a message from Kalen and instantly clicked on that. At least he gave me most of the day to relax.

Kalen: *What's up? How's spending time with you moms going? Are you still spending time with her?*

Me: *Do you miss me already? I'm currently sitting down to eat. What did you do today? Did you go and talk to Kalyla so that you two can make up?*

Kalen: *I didn't have shit to do today. I'm also not hitting her ass up first. You know her ass decided to not show up to training today. She's really doing the most, and I'm not about to go to her. Hell yeah, I missed your ass. Ya moms is going to have to spend time with you when you go home at night lol.*

Me: *You bugged out. That's your best friend, Kalen. You know how she is since you've known her for a long time. Get it together. Spending time with her is probably all she wants. It's a lot from going having you all to yourself to having to share you with me. I understand it, so you should cut her a little slack.*

Kalen: *Umm, whoever this is can you give the phone back to my girl because this isn't my girl I'm speaking to. You don't even get along with her.*

Me: *Whatever. I'm just saying I hate feeling like all of this is my fault. Y'all aren't spending time together because of me. You should have used today as a day to get right with her. Kalen, stop being stubborn.*

Kalen: *Send me a picture so I can see that I'm actually talking to my girl.*

I snapped a picture of me rolling my eyes and sent it to him.

Kalen: *Why can you never take a proper picture?*

Me: *Because I look so much better in the picture that I just sent you.*

"DiZarie? Is that you, shorty?" I heard someone call out.

I looked to the side to see Keith approaching my table.

"Oh hi," I uttered, standing to my feet.

He pulled me into a hug and inside I felt like I was doing something wrong.

"Are you here alone?" He questioned.

"Um yeah. I just decided to treat myself."

"Did you mind if I joined you or you want to be alone?" he asked.

"Um yeah, you can join me if you don't have someone else to meet," I reluctantly offered.

"Okay, no I had plans on eating alone," he expressed, sitting down.

I really didn't want him to join me, but I didn't want to be rude. Then again, I didn't really want to have dinner with him either.

"So where is your boyfriend?" Keith inquired.

"Um, at home. I had a day to myself. You know just centering DiZarie again," I informed.

He nodded his head, and the table got awkwardly silent. Everything was just uncomfortable. Then my server decided she wanted to deliver all of my food to the table at the same time. So not only was I sitting with Keith I had all this food making me look greedy as hell.

"Um, you know I just had a taste for all of this. Most will probably get bagged up and taken home with me," I said trying to make an excuse why I ordered all this food.

"You're fine. I like a girl that can eat," he joked.

"I have a man but thank you I guess." I laughed.

****

After an awkward dinner with Keith, I was frantically looking around the restaurant for my server. I needed my check and fast. For one, I felt wrong as fuck for sitting here with him eating, and then Keith was weird. I didn't like the way he looked at me, and I didn't like his conversation either. I honestly feel a little uncomfortable because through the little conversation we did have, I got the feeling that this little run in together wasn't just a lucky coincidence.

"Sorry about taking so long with your check. I tried to separate it, and the machine froze up. I just wanted to let you know they are rebooting it now, and I will get those separate checks to you." The server informed.

"Oh, no need to do separate checks. I ordered half the menu myself. Just put it on my card," I offered, handing her my debit card.

"Oh no let me pay," Keith offered.

For one I know his ass didn't really want to pay because he would have said something before when I told her separate checks the first time around. I wasn't going to point that out though. I just wanted to pay for this food and get the fuck out of here.

"Oh no! This is on me," I insisted.

He didn't fight back either. He quickly put his little prepaid card up. I went into my wallet to see if I had any cash on me to leave her a tip.

"Next time it's on me." He laughed.

I just smiled and let out a little giggle while I continued to search through my wallet. When she came back with the receipt, I quickly signed and snatching up my card while throwing down forty dollars for her tip. The bill wasn't even over fifty dollars, but I did appreciate her service. I grabbed my to-go bags said a quick by and rushed off.

"Damn, why are you in a rush?" Keith asked, grabbing my arm.

"I'm just tired and trying to get home," I lied.

"Oh, so you can spend some time with your moms?"

I froze in place hearing Kalen's voice behind me. What kind of shit is going on tonight? How in the fuck did he just so happen to end up here right now?

"Um, hey bae, what are you doing here?" I cooed, walking over to him.

That nigga didn't look happy at all. He glanced at me for a second before training his eyes back on Keith who was still standing there looking stupid as fuck. I mean like nigga read the energy and beat ya feet.

"I thought you were with your moms. This doesn't look like your moms," Kalen pointed out.

"Um, first I will say I didn't come here with him. I was alone at first."

"Were you alone all day or alone with him all day."

"If she was?" Keith spat.

"Whoa! You are way out of line. We just ran into each other here at the restaurant. I was not with him all day," I defended.

"How did you get here?" Kalen questioned still not taking his eyes off Keith.

"I drove myself," I replied, showing him my keys in hand.

"Go get in your car and meet me at my house, DiZarie. Please don't let me beat you there," Kalen gritted.

"Umm, so do I just wait in the hallways for you to come, or um do you want me to sit outside and wait? I'm not really sure what's going on right now," I rambled.

"Someone is there to let you inside!" He snapped.

Um, a part of me didn't want to listen, but I also felt the need to prove I wasn't out with him. Hopefully, Kalen didn't believe him anyway, but then again, I really didn't know. I looked between Kalen and Keith before I just decided to walk off and do what he asked. I should have never sat with this nigga.

Kalen

As soon as she turned the corner, I stalled off and knocked that nigga right in his shit. Did he really think he was going to be able to stand here and disrespect me without getting knocked in his shit?

"Aye, I don't know if she warned your ass about me before but take that as your warning. Next time your ass won't go home. Stay away from what's mine."

"Let her make the choice," he gritted, spitting blood on the ground.

"Nigga, go ahead and get fucked up behind her if you want. I see you around my girl again, and I'll do more than crack ya shit," I gritted before hopping in my car.

I needed to go somewhere to calm down. There was no way in hell she could be playing me like this. I would talk to my mother, but she always wants to be reasonable. I would talk with my Annie, but she is always going off the deep end with shit. Tonight was the night where my pops and uncles had their little fake ass meetings. Shit, I needed some good ass advice right now because I honestly want to go the fuck off on her ass. She's going to be pissed when she gets to my place and finds out who told me where the hell she was. Riah didn't know she was outing her sister's lying ass though. She told me that she out eating alone. Shit, that was the only reason why my ass popped up there, and good thing I did because I caught her ass in her lies.

****

"Yeeerrr!" I shouted out, entering Uncle Zamor's warehouse.

"Nigga, you almost got shot the fuck up playing," Uncle Zamor grunted as he lowered his gun.

I walked further into the warehouse, and all their old asses had their gun pointed at the entrance.

"The fuck y'all got going on?" I questioned, taking a seat.

"The fuck you doing here, lil nigga?" Uncle Symeer asked.

"I knew y'all old asses would be here, and I needed some advice," I admitted.

"Nigga, who the fuck you calling old? I might be getting up there in age, but I can guarantee that I can beat ya ass," Uncle Zamor challenged.

"Let me call Auntie Jana," I teased.

"Whatever, nigga. What you need advice on? If it's about ya girl, then all I can suggest is to fuck her into submission. That's how I do Jana, and that shit works every time," Zamor let out.

"That shit doesn't work because Jana is always talking shit. So damn short but got the most mouth." My pops argued.

"Don't talk about my baby. She's just passionate about shit." Zamor laughed.

"That's how you're explaining how disrespectful her ass is. Nigga y'all both belong on the little bus." Symeer chimed in laughing.

"Nigga, please shut the fuck up because you know she is still not fully fuckin' with you," Zamor pointed out.

"Can I get some advice or are y'all going to continue with this old man bickering?" I cut in.

"Damn what you need help with? Is it your girlfriend Kalyla or your actual girlfriend?" Zamor questioned.

"Kalyla is not my girlfriend. What the hell are you talking about?"

"Oh, my bad. Y'all broke up or something? You know I don't keep up with these damn relationships y'all call yourselves being in," Zamor waved.

"Um, we were never together. She is just my best friend, nothing more and nothing less. I do have some questions about her, but this is about my real life actual relationship with my girl who isn't Kalyla."

"Aight nigga, spit that shit out? What the hell happened?" Zamor rushed.

"Aight calm down. So today, my girl told me that she was going to chill with her moms today. I was like aight cool. So after training, a nigga ain't have shit to do, so I chilled around my place. Then like an hour or so ago, SJ popped up with his little girlfriend asking to chill at my place. Now, y'all know SJ's girlfriend is my girl's little sister. So, I'm like why are you not chillin' with your moms and sister. She tells me that Zarie was out eating by herself. She said something about she just wanted to be alone or some shit like that. Nevertheless, she did tell me where Zarie was eating at, so a nigga decided to pull up. I'm bored as fuck and definitely didn't want to sit around and watch SJ spit his little whack ass game. I get in my fuckin'

car and drive all the way to the restaurant only to see her ass walking

out with another nigga."

"Dammmmn, so she went out with her other boyfriend? Did

you know she had another nigga?" Zamor laughed.

"Don't do that. She doesn't have another nigga. I saw all up in

her this punk nigga's face when I went to her school before. So to

continue, she's trying to explain and say it just so happen that he was

at the same place. Then this nigga said that it wasn't. A part of me

wanted to go off on her, but then again, a part of me believed her. The

one thing I know about her is that she doesn't lie. She always says

what's on her mind and is quick to tell you when she doesn't like

something or shit just say whatever she wants. Still, all in all, she lied

about today. She wasn't out with her moms today. So should I trust

that she wasn't with this nigga all day? I mean she told me one lie

today, so who's to say she wasn't lying again," I vented.

"First off, if you think she's telling the truth, go with that. If

shorty has never lied to you before today, it has to be a good ass reason why she decided to do so today. Also, look into that nigga. I don't trust no man around my lady," Symeer advised.

"A woman will lie with a straight face. You don't know if this is her first time lying," my father added.

"Nigga don't go putting that shit in his head. He knows his girl, so don't have him second-guessing his shit with her. Talk to shorty. You will be able to tell when she's lying and when she isn't. If she were as straight up how you said she was, then it wouldn't be a problem with her telling you why she lied or if she even lied at all in the first place. Don't look too much into it because that's when shit starts getting out of hand. Be straight forward with her and talk that shit out like an adult," Symeer advised.

"Aight. Now, what about Kalyla. What's going on between the two of you? Camille has been stressing me the fuck out about that?" my father questioned, changing the whole conversation.

"Nothing is happening. She doesn't like DiZarie, and the feeling is mutual." I shrugged.

"So you stopped fuckin' with her all behind a new relationship? Damn, you and ya new girl fuckin'?" Zamor joked.

"I gave her space because she was doing the most. The day of the barbecue Kalyla was the one that extended the truce or whatever. They both agreed that even though they didn't care for each other, they could be in each other's space. Zarie didn't want to be the reason why I stopped hanging with Kalyla, so she said she would be cordial with her. Kalyla said she wanted to see me happy with someone so she would try to get to know Zarie. Not even a week later, she was on the same bullshit. It's like why even extend a truce or an agreement if you knew you weren't going to be able to do it. So, I'm trying to prevent some shit from poppin' off because of your WIFE!" I snapped, pointing at uncle Symeer.

"My wife what?" He questioned.

"So, Zarie is talking to Annie telling her how she tried with Kalyla, and she wasn't about to do too much more of Kalyla playing in her face."

"Ohh okay, say no more. I already know what the advice was," Symeer cut in.

"What was the advice?" My father asked.

"You know Nyrae. She feels like everything can be solved with her putting hands on someone. So, I know for sure it was along those lines," Symeer answered.

"That's exactly what she advised. Actually, Zarie expressed wanting to do that, and Annie encouraged her. So, Zarie told me she would try, but Kalyla refuses to be around her. I went to talk with her you know to get her to agree to come chill with us and shit, but she wasn't trying to do it. Like what else did she want me to do? I'm not trying to push her out of my life, but she had to know that eventually we were going to get with someone and shit would change between us."

"So are you sure it's not your girl telling you not to be around Kalyla?" Zamor questioned.

"Nah, she's been trying to get me to talk and fix shit with Kalyla. I'm just not with it. I didn't do anything wrong," I defended.

"Hell nah! She ain't trying to get you to fix anything." Zamor laughed.

I pulled out my phone and showed them the multiple times Zarie has tried to get me to talk to Kalyla. I didn't want them thinking she was one of those girls because she's far from it.

"Okay, so I guess she's a good one. Why you here questioning her if she knows shorty is solid?" Zamor asked still scrolling through my shit.

I sat up and snatched my phone back because he was doing too much scrolling.

"Nigga, go home and talk with shorty. Also, go and talk with Kalyla like shorty has been suggesting. You two have a history and this new girl even though she's cool shouldn't be coming in between the two of you," my father scolded.

"Do you not like my girl or something?" I snapped.

"I'm just saying Camille pointed out some shit, and it's looking like what she had to say is true. Step back from shorty and get your home front fixed up!" he spat.

"What's with everyone against me having a shorty? Shorty has done nothing but try to fix shit, but I'm the one against it. At the end of the day, Kalyla needs to accept the fact that she can't have all of my time. It's not like I'm talking about some unbelievable shit. If she thought that we were going to get into a relationship with people and still spend all our time together that's her fault. All in all, I didn't dismiss her from my life, but that was her choice."

"So, you are willing to risk it all for this girl?" My pops asked for clarification.

"What am I risking? I am not shutting Kalyla out. This is her choice not to be around me. She's not my main priority. Why does it seem like everyone is lost on that idea? She isn't my shorty and to be honest she will never be. So what's up, are we going to continue to have this problem if my relationship continues with DiZarie or if I get someone new? It doesn't matter. She still won't be a choice! What the fuck am I going to do then? It's pissing me off that y'all taking her side in this shit and not thinking about the fact of me not wanting to be with her! Man, coming here was definitely a mistake. Aye Unc, appreciate the advice. I needed that. I'm about to head back to the crib to deal with my shorty," I announced, standing to my feet.

"So are you about to just shut out everyone for this girl?" My pops barked.

"What the hell is wrong with y'all? Is it really that bad that I'm with someone? Nothing has changed. It's like everyone hates my girl but Annie and P. Storm."

"Storm met shorty, and he likes her? Maybe it is something wrong with y'all. You know that old nigga doesn't like nobody," Zamor cut in.

"Bring her around the family more. Maybe we can get a different opinion of her," my pops suggested.

"Um, I'm good for now. It's best to only have her around people that likes her. Yeah, I'm out of here," I announced before walking off.

****

"Ooo Zarie, you in trouble now." I heard Riah laugh.

SJ was knocked out sleep on my damn couch, and I'm assuming Zarie and her sister was back in my room.

"Riah, I didn't do anything wrong. What the hell do I look like being into Keith? I didn't even want him joining my table. I hope

Kalen doesn't think something more happened or that I was with him all day. That is far from the truth," Zarie whined.

"So, you really like Kalen? Normally you wouldn't even care. You actually listened to him and have been in here shook waiting for him to come back. He's probably down the hall with his other girlfriend."

"Oh, bitch, don't play like that. Yes, I like him, which is the only reason why I feel like I need to explain myself. Do you think he will believe me? I mean I just felt like I needed a little me time. With mommy all in my ear and me always being with Kalen, I just wanted to chill. Me trying to be anti today can result in my boyfriend leaving me. Ugh, relationships are so hard," Zarie groaned.

I shook my head at how dramatic she was being. Walking into my room the both of them turned around, and instantly Zarie poked out her bottom lip.

"Pick ya lip up." I laughed kicking my shoes off.

Riah got up from the bed and left out the room.

"I hope you're not mad at me," she groaned.

I stared at her for a second before turning to my dresser to empty my pockets. Out of the corner of the mirror, I could see her watching my every move. I wanted to laugh, but she needed to see that I was still pissed that she was out eating with other niggas.

"So that was spending time with ya moms, huh?" I questioned, turning around and leaning against my dresser.

"No! I actually spent the day alone," she admitted.

"Oh wow! So, the whole day was a lie."

"I mean my mother did complain about not spending time with me. I see her when I go home, so she was really was being dramatic. So, I took the day to get myself together. I did yoga. You know I took a nice long bath. I went shopping and then to eat."

"So, if you wanted to chill by yourself why not just say that? Why did you lie?"

"Because you have a way of talking me into things I don't want to do. It was hard for me to tell you and your grandfather no earlier. I just needed to relax and spoil myself for the day."

"What else don't you want to do and you're not telling me?" I inquired.

"Um, even though the training is fun, I don't want to go to anymore. I don't know what your grandfather is trying to turn me into, but like I'm good on all that," she added.

"Is that all?"

"Um, also I was only trying to be nice when I allowed Keith to sit at my table. I didn't even get to really eat all my food. It was very uncomfortable, and he's weird," she added.

"Anything else?"

"Um, it was rude as fuck for you to have me sitting here this long waiting for you to get here."

"Anything else?" I asked, laughing.

"Yeah, you can tell me you aren't mad at me. Then we can lay together and um I don't know. Just don't be mad at me."

I stood there with my arms folded across my chest. There sat a beautiful girl with her untamed hair all over her head. I believed her, but I don't know.

DiZarie

I didn't know what else I could say to make him believe me. I know I lied about what I did for the day, but Keith wasn't even worth lying about. He took his shirt off and then his pants as he walked over to the bed. He climbed under his sheets and just laid there staring at the ceiling. He was really giving me the silent treatment right now. I followed suit and climbed under the covers too. Kalen cut his eyes on me and went back to staring straight ahead.

"Kalen!" I cooed.

He turned his head in my direction and gave me a blank stare. I sucked my teeth and rolled my eyes before climbing on top of him. This was definitely out of my comfort zone.

"Am I heavy?" I asked, staring down at him.

He shook his head no and just smirked.

"Are you going to speak to me? Or are we going to continue this whole awkward exchange?"

He shrugged his shoulders and laughed. I leaned down, and he gave me a questioning look.

"Do you forgive me?" I asked, kissing his lips.

"Why should I?" he questioned, kissing me again.

"Because I just want you to forgive me. I don't like the silent treatment. Also, look how long it took me to tolerate you. You know I don't have the patience to deal with another nigga, especially not Keith," I scoffed.

"Nigga, you are not in the position to be talking shit right now, talking about tolerating me." He laughed.

"Ugh, you know what I mean."

"Aye, get up right quick," he called out, tapping my hip.

"Why am I heavy?" I quizzed.

"Nah, I um…"

"I already felt it, so there is no need to try and hide it now." I laughed.

"Nah, because yo ass like playing. You rub yo ass on me and shit while you sleep and have a nigga looking like a perv in the morning and shit," he argued.

"Don't blame that on me. You always all up on me. What do you think will happen?" I defended.

He grabbed my hips to keep me still, and I felt his full erection. He looked in my eye and then gave me a knowing look.

"Exactly get ya ass up."

Kalen wasn't about to play me like I couldn't handle it because that was far from the truth. I stood to my feet and started to undress. Kalen laid eye widen as he laid back on the bed and watched me closely.

"You don't have to do this," he called out.

"You know when it comes to my body that I don't do anything I don't want to do."

He just nodded his head in agreement. He knew one thing I would never compromise on is who I am as a woman. I would never do anything that would make me feel objectified or was degrading, so

I don't even know why he said that. My shorts and shirt were off as I slowly got back on my knees.

"Can we do this my way?" I asked smirking.

"What you mean your way? You're not a virgin?" he spat, sitting up.

"No, I'm not. Did you get with me thinking I'm a virgin?"

"No, I just didn't think you were… I mean you know how you are so hung up about not being looked at for your body. I thought you weren't fuckin'."

"Just because I appreciate a man that loves my mind before my body doesn't mean I don't like being pleased. Now are we going to do this my way or is this going to be boring?"

"Ain't shit about fuckin' me is boring. You better do some next level shit. You got all this damn mouth, so let's see what's up." He smirked.

That's all I needed to hear. I went to grab my phone, and I unlocked to go to my music to create a quick playlist. I could feel his eyes on me, but I don't care. He will see. I finished with my quick little playlist and just when I was about to send it to him, I saw my sister texted me saying that she and SJ left and he was taking her home.

"Where's your phone?" I questioned with my hand out.

He passed it to me, and I shared the playlist. I got up and went to grab his headphones along with something to cover his eyes.

"Hell nah, you not about to tie me up. What the fuck do you think this is?" he disputed.

"Sit up on the edge of the bed, please. I'm not going to tie you up."

"What the fuck are you trying to do then?" he asked, giving me an unsure look.

"It's so we can have an experience," I smirked.

I held both of our phones up to show him the playlist, and I saw a little smirk appear on his face.

"I'm going to cover your eyes, and we both will listen to the same playlist in the same order. You will have your headphones in." I instructed.

"Hell nah. How do I know it's going to be you? You are not about to get me." He laughed shaking his head no.

"Kalen, who else will do this? I'm standing in front of you right now in nothing but my underwear," I replied, holding my arms out.

"Take the rest off," he demanded.

"Take it off of me," I purred.

"Are you serious right now?"

I nodded my head like duh. He grabbed my arm and pulled my body toward him. I yelped out in shock. Our lips connected as his hands slowly slid up my back unhooking my bra. My straps falling down my arms didn't stop anything. My bra dropped to the floor and his hands went to my ass. Pulling me closer to his body he massaged my ass with his large hands. Slowly my panties were being pulled down.

His lips when from my lips down yo my neck. Kalen licked and sucked on my neck, causing a soft moan to escape my lips.

"Hmmm!" I moaned out.

His tongue trailed from my neck down to my nipples. Kalen licked, sucked, and used his teeth to gently pull and bite on my nipples. My hands were on the back of his head pushing my breasts into his mouth.

"You sure you want to take the lead." He laughed standing up.

He pulled my hair causing my head to go back. He placed soft kisses at the corner of my mouth and began his teasing trail again.

"Hmmm!" I moaned out.

This was not going as I planned. My nails were clawing at his lower back. He stopped at stared down at me. The lust was definitely apparent in his eyes. I know for sure that my eyes mirrored the same look. He laid back on the bed, and I stood stuck for a second.

"Climb up here and squat above my face," he ordered.

"What?" I stammered.

"You heard what I said," he proclaimed.

This was supposed to be my show right now, but I wasn't about dispute feeding my nigga. I climbed onto the bed, and he motioned for me to come towards his face. I glanced at the door to make sure it was locked. I let out a shaky breath and squatted over his face.

"Damn, you smell good," he groaned in between my legs.

He locked his arms around my thighs bringing my pussy closer to his face. As soon as his tongue invaded my fold, I moaned out in pleasure. My back straightening with my eyes closed.

"Fuck!" I moaned out.

Marveling in each stroke of his tongue, I grind my pussy in his face as he continued to assault my pearl. He took his hand and slapped my ass hard as hell. He stuck his tongue in my hole and ran his tongue back up to my clit. He repeated the action, and I couldn't even contain my moans. He slapped my ass again. Oddly enough, that made me moan louder.

"Hmmmm, Kalen!" I moaned.

He locked me down where I couldn't move his lips locked around my clit.

"Ughh Kalen, I'm about to cum!" I screeched.

He continued to feast on my pussy. My legs were shaking as he continued to assault my pussy with his tongue. I let out a shaky breath, and I released. I was still locked in as he licked up all my nectar. When he finished, I tried to move, but his ass wasn't letting up. He kissed my pussy and let me go. I fell to the side, and he got up laughing.

"And you wanted to run the show?" He laughed again kissing my neck.

"That's not funny. I never did that before. Now if I had started this off, it would have been different. Give me a minute and watch," I warned.

"Hell nah, you go the next go around. I'm not done yet," he exclaimed, opening my legs.

I thought it was going to be a little break but his ass was already out of his underwear. He grabbed his dick and positioned himself at my opening. I wasn't ready, but when he was pushing through my tight walls, I moaned out in pleasure. Oh, he can definitely take over my body.

****

The Next Day

I was showered and in some of Kalen's clothes. He had to go to training, and I was not doing that again, so I was about to head home. My moms had already texted me about not telling her that I was staying with Kalen. She was going have to stop all of this. Here I am twenty-one years old and she always on my back about where I am.

"I'll talk to you later," Kalen said standing at my car.

"Alright later," I agreed.

He kissed my lips and opened my door for me to get in. I got in and started up my car to leave. As I was looking in my rearview mirror to back out, I saw all my shopping bags from yesterday. I didn't even need Kalen's clothes.

Ring, Ring, Ring!

I saw it was my mother calling. I rolled my eyes and accepted the call.

"DiZarie!" my mother yelled into the line.

"Ugh, ma! Why are you screaming like that? Yes?" I groaned.

"Why do you keep testing me? What is so hard about you coming home at night? This shit is getting out of hand now!" she snapped.

"Ma, something happened yesterday, and we had to talk. I fell asleep again, and I am on my way home now. Besides, I'm twenty-one. When do I have to stop telling you if I'm coming home or not," I sassed.

"And you telling me y'all aren't fuckin'. There is no way y'all are just sleeping. Are you having sex with him? Also, you stop telling me when you aren't living under my roof anymore!" she snapped.

"I'm on my way home. I should be there in another ten minutes. I'm coming home and going right to sleep. I won't sleep out without telling you again," I replied.

"I see how you tried not to answer my question. I'll see you when you get here!" my momma spat hanging up.

Raniya wasn't about to work my nerves with this being on me about staying out.

****

"Daddy is looking for you!" Riah laughed as she came into my room jumping on my bed.

"Ugh, what does he want? I'm trying to go to sleep. It's too earlier for all of this," I groaned getting under my covers.

"You know ya momma told him you been out. If you want some suggestions, I suggest staying under the covers or putting on a sweater. I saw those hickies." Riah teased.

"Ugh!!! Tell him in sleep, or I'm on my period. You know he hates talking to us during that time. I don't have time for the questions!" I snapped running into my bathroom.

I looked at the marks that decorated my skin and rolled my eyes. What the hell was I looking at this morning because this wasn't there after the shower I had at his place, or maybe it was, and I just wasn't pay attention.

"Was this your first time?" Riah asked, smiling.

"With him? Yeah," I replied, touching the marks

"What do you mean with him? You've had sex with someone else before? Why didn't I know? How was it? Why don't you talk to me about these things?" She pouted.

"Go make sure daddy doesn't come in here and we can talk about whatever," I offered.

"Bet!" she replied running out my bathroom and room.

I rolled my eyes laughing because her ass was being extra. I grabbed my phone as I climbed back into the bed. When the light came on it showed a text from Kalen. With a smile on my face, I clicked the phone to read his message. That smile was quickly washed away.

Kalen: *I hope you got home safely.*

Kalen: *I never knew that me falling for you would cause these many problems in other people's lives. The night we shared with each other solidified what I've been feeling for you and made me realize that no matter how much I believe you're perfect for me, it will still cause too many problems in our lives. Since we got together, it's like only two people in my family are willing to accept you. Each day it's like I'm being hit with some new bullshit. I think that right now it's best if we step away from each other for a while so that I can get some* *shit straight. This shit seems so fucked up as I text this message, but I hope you know me well enough to know that this wasn't done on no heartless shit. I'm feeling the fuck outta you DiZarie, but right now it's just not our time.*

I sat up in my bed with my mouth dropped open. I can't believe he was doing this right now. He couldn't come to this conclusion last night before we fucked? I felt so fuckin' stupid right now. Did this nigga have this plan all along? This is what I get for even thinking about dating. I should have gone with my initial instinct. I should have stayed away from him. Here it is my feelings are all caught up in this nigga and our bullshit ass relations. All it took was a simple ass text for him to have everything stop. How could I be so stupid? How could I open my legs for him? How did I not see this coming? Did I ignore the signs? This nigga really fucked me and broke up with me through text the next day. Wo!

Me: *Wow! You come to that realization quick. You couldn't say that in my face this morning. You are definitely a lesson learned. Thank you and fuck you!*

I held my phone in my hand tightly as I tried to calm myself down. This nigga really played me like this.

"Ahhhh!!!" I screamed out before forcefully throwing my phone against the wall.

Fuck all of this shit and fuck Kalen!

Kalyla

T he day I told Zobie that I was leaving, I can admit I was being overdramatic. No, I didn't leave to go to my father, but I did stop going to training. The only person that came to check on me was Zobie. I give him a hard time, but he has definitely been showing me he cared about me. I haven't spoken to Kalen since the time he came to my place and called himself going off on me. I wasn't in the business of chasing his ass down. He wanted to be with her then so be it.

I was currently in my kitchen cooking because Zobie said he was coming over after he finished with training. If he went in on time, he was going to show up to my place at any time. So when he got here, the food would be hot. I fried up some wingettes and tossed them in the dry ranch seasoning to make some bomb ass, ranch wings. For sides, I made some tater tots because I loved those and some Velveeta shells and cheese because Zobie ass can buss down a whole pot by himself.

All this time I've been spending with Zobie, it was like being around Kalen. However, with Zobie I had a pretty clear idea of what

I wanted to happen between us. We kiss a lot, but he wouldn't go all the way there with me. This felt like a little kid relationship. I've asked him multiple times what are we, but his ass has been ducking and dodging the question. However, today he was definitely going to answer that question.

I shook the thought of Zobie playing with me out of my head and finished cooking the last bit of food. Once everything was done, and the stove was off, I rushed to the back to hop in the shower. I did not want him coming here, and I smell like chicken grease and tater tots. That ain't sexy at all.

****

"Aye! Kalyla, where you at shorty?" I heard in my living room.

I had just finished putting on my little shorts, so I slid my feet into my house shoes and rushed out to the living room. I was about to ask him how the hell he got inside my house when I saw Kalen standing in my living room too.

"What the fuck you got on?" Zobie questioned staring me up and down as he made his way over to me.

I was still stuck on Kalen being inside my place. I hope his little bitch wasn't coming too. Rolling my eyes at Kalen, I hugged and kissed Zobie on the lips before trying to walk off to the kitchen.

"Shorty, go put some pants on," he demanded.

"I have on shorts," I defended.

"Yo, you really got ya ass hanging out. Go out some pants on," He reiterated.

"It's just Kalen! Why do I have to change?" I argued.

"Don't no man want his shorty parading around half dressed in front of another nigga," he disputed.

"Um, when…"

He cut his eyes at me, and I stopped talking and turned on my heels to put on some pants. He got that now but when we were alone, I was definitely going to figure out when he became my nigga. I slipped on a pair of sweatpants and went back out into the living room. I saw Zobie in the kitchen making his plate, and Kalen sitting on the couch looking like his world was over. He wasn't my concern, so I went into the kitchen and tried to make Zobie's plate.

"I got this. Go in there and talk with Kalen. I hope you feel bad after this talk too," he chastised shooting me out my kitchen.

"Um, why do I need to speak to him? I didn't ask him to come here. My life has been going on just fine since he hasn't been in it," I disputed, rolling my eyes.

"Kalyla," he gritted.

I sucked my teeth and went into the living room. I sat on the couch and stared at the side of his face. He was all in his phone looking at a text message.

"So what's wrong with you?" I asked.

"I'm good," he replied.

"No, you are not! What happened to you? Where is your little girlfriend?" I taunted.

"Don't fuckin' do that. Everyone has a little fuckin' problem with my relationship, so I'm not in one anymore. It's just life, right?" he asked dully.

"I knew you two wouldn't last. Don't blame that on me. I tried to save you from this."

"You serious right now?" he barked.

"Yeah, I'm serious!" I yelled back.

"Yo, that's fucked up that you don't give a fuck about a nigga wanting to be happy and shit. You had my whole family looking at me like I was flaw as fuck because I wanted to be with shorty. She made sense to me. I loved being around her. We had that homie and lover type shit. We couldn't have a peaceful relationship without everyone putting your fuck ass feelings before mine. You had my whole family telling me I was wrong for being with someone, and you don't see a problem with that. That's fuckin' crazy. But of course, you get what you want. I honestly came over here to tell you that you didn't have to bitch anymore. You have all my time now. I'm about to get out of here," he announced, getting up from the couch.

He walked over to my front door and opened it to leave. Before he walked out the door, he took the key to my place and threw it on the floor. I swear Kalen is so fuckin' dramatic. Zobie walked into the living with two plates in his hands. He sat my plate in front of me and moved to a different couch to sit down.

"What's wrong with you?" I pressed.

"I heard what the fuck you said. You're a piece of work shorty. Don't nothing good come to a selfish mothafucka. You not giving one fuck that he went and gave up on a girl that he was really feeling has me looking at you sideways. That's some real fucked up shit, Kalyla," he snarled.

"Well, I didn't tell him to break up with that girl, Zobie. I haven't spoken to him," I defended.

"That's because you walk around acting like your fuckin' life is over. You refuse to act like a fuckin' adult. What kind of best friend are you? A shitty ass best friend. I don't see how that nigga dealt with you all this time," he sneered.

"Wow! You saying all this like you didn't just say you were my nigga. How are you my nigga but you want to look down on me? You have to choose one, Zobie," I sassed.

"I choose not to be bothered with you. That's fucked up that you don't care about your friends. That's real selfish, and I feel like with you being twenty one a grown ass woman I shouldn't be telling you some shit like this."

I huffed and got up from the couch grabbing my keys. I stomped out of my place and all the way to Kalen's place. Placing my key in the door, it didn't work. *Damn, he changed his locks too?*

Knock, Knock, Knock!

"What?" He snapped, opening the door.

"Damn, I can't come in?"

"Nah, I'm not in the mood for company. What's going on?" he asked, still guarding his door.

"Well, I came to tell you that you didn't have to break up with that girl because of me. We weren't talking, so I don't even get why you did that."

"Even though we weren't talking, everyone else still had something to say. Your fuck ass moms that can't stay out of our business, and then there is my fuck ass father. Everyone is taking your side like I completely pushed you out of my life, and we both know that's not what happened. You got what you wanted. My time isn't being divided between you and her. It's all yours. Just call me before showing up to my place," he ranted before slamming the door in my face.

He was doing the absolute most right now. He will calm down, and everything will finally be back to normal between us. Kalen just needed to get over that little ex-girlfriend of his and the world will be a better place. Kalen was just taking things to the extreme right now. I honestly don't get why he's acting so hurt behind ole girl. She wasn't that great. I shrugged my shoulders and walked on back down to my apartment.

"You can't say I didn't try," I sassed as soon as I stepped foot into my apartment.

Zobie just shook his head in disappointment and continued eating his food.

DiZarie

Four Months Later

I was irritated and completely over the day. The rest of the summer was some shit, and I did nothing but sit in the house. I was now back in school, and it almost didn't happen. Right before the fall semester started, I got the shock of my life. Not only did Kalen bitch ass break up with me over text, but he also left his little swimmers behind too. I had no plans on keeping this baby or telling anyone that I was pregnant. Auntie Riah saved this baby life because if her ass didn't catch me looking at the results, I would have gone to the chop shop. Her ass ran to go tell my mother, and once she found out, that was it.

Two Months Earlier

I stood in my bathroom looking at the four different pregnancy tests that I took. What kind of luck do I have? I was so close to getting my degree, and honestly, my life was just getting back on track. Now here it is another roadblock being thrown at me. I swiped the other test off the counter and sat on the floor of my bathroom crying my eyes out. All of this was just a fucked up situation. I was already planning

Chosen: Forever & A Day with My Brooklyn Bae

on what to do next in my head because becoming a single mother was not on the list of goal I had.

"What's that? Zarie, are you pregnant?" I heard from behind me.

I glanced over my shoulder to see Riah standing there with her mouth dropped open.

"Don't worry. I am not keeping this baby," I admitted.

"Wait. What? You can't get rid of your baby, DiZarie! Mommy and daddy will not go for that," she disputed.

"I don't care what they will go for. I am twenty-one, and I can get that done on my own. The fuck I look like having a baby by a nigga that played me. I have a goal to reach and being a baby mama to a fuck nigga is not on my list of goals." I snapped.

"MAAAAAA! Nah, you bugging right now. You are only doing that because you still hurt behind Kalen. I know he messed up, but don't take that out on my niece," she accused.

"You can't tell me what's going to happen to my body," I argued.

E. Shanie

"What's going on in here?" my mother asked.

I quickly tried to hide the pregnancy tests that were scattered over my bathroom floor. It was too late though my mother already had one in her hands.

"DiZarie," she cooed in a disapproving tone.

"Ma," was all I got out before I covered my face with my hands and broke down into tears. This was never supposed to be my life.

"You told me you weren't fuckin'. Don't cry now." She laughed.

"Ma, that's not funny!" I yelled, crying harder.

"Well, what do you want DiZarie? You can't get rid of this baby."

"Why not? I don't want a kid. I'm not finished school." I cried.

"Well, that will not stop you. You have us to help."

"Noooooo, I want my daddy," I cried, getting up the floor and getting in my bed.

"He's at work, and you can talk to me. You are being dramatic right now."

"Nooo MA!! I want my daddy. Uggghh," I bawled.

"Oh, you're serious right now. Okay, stop all that loud crying, DiZarie. I'm calling him right now," my mother assured.

That definitely didn't stop me from crying. I cannot believe this. I just needed my daddy right now, and he will tell me what to do. He can assure me that everything will be okay.

"De just get here so that you can get her to stop crying. She too old for this shit honestly," I mother murmured.

"Ma, I didn't ask you to come in here!" I snapped from under the covers.

"Yeah, you're trying me. Here your daddy wants to talk to you," my mother informed me, sticking her phone under my comforter.

"What's wrong, baby girl?" my daddy asked.

Like a little girl, I cried into the phone talking trying to tell him what was wrong with me.

"Zarie. Calm down what is going on with you?" my daddy cooed.

"I-I-I... I don't want a baby," I cried.

"Wait, excuse me?"

"Kalen broke up with me through a text, and now I'm having a babyyyyy! Daddy, I can't do this," I cried.

"Well, that's too late to say don't you think. You will be fine. Having a baby will not change your life. You can still finish school. I'm going to wrap it up here, and I'll be home in a little bit," he assured.

"Okay," I whined.

He disconnected the call, and I stuck my arm out and threw my mothers phone on the floor.

"DiZarie! You are really trying me, child. You will get your ass beat pregnant and all," my mother threatened.

"Oh my gosh! My life is hard enough as it is. Ma, please get out! Oh and Riah don't go tell your little boyfriend my business either.

This does not need to be discussed outside of this house," I warned coming from under the covers to make sure she understood me.

She nodded her head in agreement. That was all I needed to see I plopped back onto my bed and went to go cry underneath my covers.

That day my father came home and let me cry in his arms. He was a little upset, I could tell, but he made sure he assured me that everything was going to be okay. For a little while, I still considered getting an abortion, but after doing some research, I saw that I would still be able to take the last bit of classes so I can get my Biochemistry degree. I had three different chemistry classes, and I just wanted to make sure I could be in those classes during pregnancy. Everything was all good. Well, I really ignored it for the most part until recently. I was now four months along and unfortunately showing.

This little baby bump was just like a constant fuck you in my face from Kalen's bitch ass. I changed my thoughts from Kalen as I walked into the house. I wondered who was here because a car that I didn't recognize was outside. Instead of going to find out, I went upstairs to strip out of the extra clothes and then back down the steps to the kitchen in a pair of leggings and a camisole.

"Ma! Dr. Best really tried to put me out of class today. She had the nerve to look at me and tell me she didn't know I was expecting when in fact I had a talk with all my professors, including her ugly behind. I even took the print outs that showed I could take those classes. This little baby bump has started showing and now she wants to act funny. If she tries to make me drop my class, I am going to tear that school up," I vented, looking through the fridge.

When I closed the door and looked towards the table, I froze in place. There sat my mother, my daddy, Riah, SJ, Nyrae, and her husband. Wow, so no one thought to text me and give me a heads up. I didn't know what to say, so I just turned to leave out the kitchen.

"NOPE! Wait a minute!" Ms. Nyrae called out.

I stopped in my tracks and turned to face her.

"Kalen did not tell me you were expecting! Wait, I also haven't seen you two together? Is this his baby? How far along are you?" she questioned, reaching out touching my little growing bump.

"Um, this is my baby. I don't fuck with Kalen, so it's none of his business. Is there anything else you want to know?" I snapped.

"Oh, well excuse me. I thought we were cool. What happened?" Nyrae questioned, sizing me up.

"Yeah, I'm taking my anger out on the wrong person, but this is my baby, and I am four months along. Unfortunately, Kalen is the father, but he will not be a part of my child's life." I concluded.

"Wait a second now. You can't do that. Why can't he be there?" Nyrae argued.

"Well, because the last time I checked I was a complication to his life and he longer wanted to see me. He made his choice, and I'm fine with it."

"What do you mean he said you complicate his life?" she wondered.

"He texted me the day after we slept together and said and I quote *'it seems like only two people in my family accepts you'*, which is you and your dad. Anyway, he also said something to the effect that what everyone else had to say about what we had was more important than our actual relationship. So yeah, he didn't care when he decided to break up with me through text, so I figured he wouldn't care about this. I would love to keep this to myself."

"Um, you know I can't do that. Thanks for telling me this though. He will get handled. Take my number down because I would love to get updates on the baby. I'll even go to doctors appointments with you, if you will allow me," Nyrae offered.

I stared at her blankly before giving her my number and walking off to my room. She can tell Kalen whatever she wants, but he couldn't get in contact with me. I know for sure my mother and father weren't letting him in this house to talk to me. He was also blocked from all sources of communications. FUCK KALEN!

Kalen

I t was like everything went back to normal. I stupidly forgave Kalyla, and we went on like everything was all good. She didn't bring up DiZarie, and I didn't either. I had my bitch moments though and would look at pictures of her and shit that I had in my phone. SJ would give me updates on what she had going on in her life. That shit wasn't doing anything for me. I swear if I knew I could pick shit up where we left it off at, I would have been happy as fuck to stop being around Kalyla. This shit really pissed a nigga off that she can fuckin' laugh and joke around with a nigga like she didn't give a fuck about what I had to give up just to fuckin' hang out with her ass.

Kalyla still saw no faults in her ways. That shit was crazy, but hey, nobody was fuckin' complaining telling me I was going against the fam.

"Ahh Kalen, did you hear what he said," Kalyla laughed, leaning on my shoulder.

I just stared tirelessly at the TV screen. Shit, I couldn't even tell you what the fuck we were watching. She placed her hand on my chest and moved closer to me. I shrugged her off and created a little space between us.

"What's wrong with you?" Kalyla asked, scooting closer to me.

"You're all up in my personal space. Damn, can a nigga get some space?" I snapped.

"Damn, we use to do this all the time. All of a sudden, I can't be close to you. What's the problem with you?" she inquired.

"It's no problem over here. I just don't want you all on me. The fuck you want me to say. We can watch TV without you all up on me. What's going on with you?" I asked suspiciously.

"There is nothing wrong with me. It's you that's acting up," she replied, touching the middle of my sweats.

"Whoa! Oh, you wilding out right now. The fuck kind of shit you on, Lyla?" I barked standing up.

"I need to know what I want. It's either I have feelings for you, or it's really for Zobie. If we kiss—"

"OH HELL NO! The fuck I look like kissing you. That will never happen. I've said this to everybody, and I know I've said this to you before too. I am not into you like that. I see you as a sister and nothing more. I don't know what kind of vibe I'm…"

Bang, Bang, Bang, Bang!

Who the fuck is banging on my door like that? I pushed pass Kalyla who stood there looking stupid and yanked my door open ready to go off. In came a pissed off Annie, and I was confused as fuck.

"I cannot fuckin' believe you, Kalen. You were raised better than that. This fuckin' girl has to go through this all alone because you decided on being a fuck nigga!" my Annie shouted, mushing me.

"What are you talking about?" I questioned confusingly.

"You broke up with her in a text message! What kind of heartless shit is that? I know I've told your ass multiple times that what other mothafuckas don't agree with doesn't change your gah damn life. You wanted to be with that girl but because Kalyla wanted to whine and act like a fuckin' brat you give up your relationship. Kalen, I can call you a lot of things, but I never thought I would call you a fuckin' idiot. Not only are you going to miss out on an amazing girl, but you're going to miss out on being in your child's life. You now have to deal with the fact that this girl can hold this against you forever and be bitter and not allow you around your child. I mean we can fight it, but shit, I would be doing the same thing if I was her!" my Annie barked.

"I am so confused right now. What are you talking about?"

"DiZarie is four months pregnant. Your stupid ass over here chillin' with someone who doesn't give a fuck about you and you're risking it all!" my Annie snapped, slapping me in the back of my head.

"Wait. What?" I asked for clarification.

"You got her pregnant?" Kalyla asked with tears in her eyes.

To Be Continued….

To submit a manuscript for our review email us at

kellzkpublishing@gmail.com

Join our mailing list to get a notification when Kellz K Publishing has another release!

Text KKP to 22828 to join

CPSIA information can be obtained
at www.ICGtesting.com
Printed in the USA
LVHW031935010419
612563LV00001B/125/P

9 781090 640963